SKIN

SKIN

a novel by DONNA JO NAPOLI

SKYSCAPE

Text copyright © 2013 by Donna Jo Napoli

Amazon Publishing
Attn: Amazon Children's Publishing
P.O. Box 400818
Las Vegas, NV 89140
www.amazon.com/amazonchildrenspublishing

Library of Congress Cataloging-in-Publication Data TK

ISBN-13: 9781477817216 (hardcover)
ISBN-10: 1477817212 (hardcover)
ISBN-13: 9781477816905 (paperback)
ISBN-10: 1477816909 (paperback)
ISBN-13: 9781477867211 (eBook)
ISBN-10: 147786721X (eBook)

Book design by Abby Kuperstock
Editor: Melanie Kroupa

Printed in the United States of America (R)
First edition
10 9 8 7 6 5 4 3 2

For Noam, sine qua non.

SKIN

MY LIPS ARE WHITE.

This can't be happening. The first day of school? People have panic dreams about this sort of thing, but they don't really happen. Giant zits happen. Bad hair happens. White lips—nuh uh, no way.

I rub the sleep from my eyes. I wash my face and brush my teeth and part my hair and clip it. One clip on each side right above my ears. I look ready. Almost . . .

My lips are still white.

Yesterday—when totally no one but my family saw me—my lips were, well, lip-colored. That's what they were all day. That's what they were last night.

Now, here in the bathroom, looking in the mirror, on a morning when everyone will see me, they are white. White.

I touch them. They feel like they've always felt. And nothing comes off on my fingers. It is not white powder or white chalk or anything like that. It is not a magic lightbulb, or the rest of me would look weird, too. My brother Dante did not play some trick on me in the night.

It's not a bad trip, because I don't do drugs.

And it is not a dream. I'm completely awake. I smell breakfast. Unmistakable. Dad is making Dutch pancake—one big giant thing that fills a twelve-inch diameter iron frying pan and rises up like half a beach ball, then falls when he takes it out of the oven. But falling is what it's supposed to do. It's delicious.

I drop my head and inspect my feet. I cut my toenails last night and scrubbed away the green stains from walking barefoot in the grass this summer. My feet are ready. I'm dressed, so I can't check the rest of me, but I know I'm ready. Let my face be ready. Please.

I look at the mirror again. White lips. Mirrors don't lie: my lips are white.

I am not a white girl. That is, I am a white girl, or sort of. I'm a Mediterranean mutt, but mostly Italian, which means I get classified as Caucasian on forms that ask for race. Last year, Owen said we should all just write human for race. So at the start of tenth grade, a bunch of us put human on the health form. Mr. Eberly, the head counselor, made us all change it.

Whatever. I am Caucasian. Italian style. I have a Roman nose, like my grandfather Nonno. And thick lips, and big cheeks. My skin is deep olive-brown by the end of summer, and it is now the end of summer; the first day of school makes that official, regardless of the calendar. Even in the middle of winter, though, I am not white. I become a kind of pale green. Sort of sickly looking. But not white.

Besides, even white girls—peaches and cream girls—don't have white lips.

Am I delusional? The first day of school and I've lost my mind. Perfect.

"Slut, get out of the bathroom."

That's Dante. His latest joy seems to be calling me slut. I am as far from a slut as anyone gets. Even my best friend Devin has kissed more boys than me. But Dante calls me it for three reasons. One, he thinks he's a riot. Two, he's proud he's finally found a nickname for me that trumps the one I have for him—which is Squirt. Three, he knows I hate it. I want to punch him. But I'm not a puncher.

"That's it, Slut. I'm coming in."

I have barely enough time to put my palm over my mouth before Dante barges in.

I rush out as he's lifting the toilet seat with one hand and blowing his nose into the other. My brother is so nasty. It is astoundingly unfair that my totally unpoetic brother got the name Dante.

And I got Giuseppina. There's no excuse for my parents naming me that. I mean, they're not complete morons.

There is no nice nickname for Giuseppina. You can't take the first syllable because that would sound like you were calling me Jew. You can't take the last two syllables (even though my parents do) because that sounds too much like *penis*. People laugh when they hear my parents call me that.

Anyway, I go by Sep, which is as close to the center of my name as it can be. But I pronounce it with a Z at the start. Kids think it's okay. Very few people know my real name. Devin and Owen do, of course. They know just about everything about me. But I can't think who else does, outside my family. I'm careful to write a note to every teacher every fall asking them please never to use my full name in class.

So, my name sucks.

And now I have white lips.

When I am twenty-one I can change my name.

But these white lips can't wait that long.

"LOOK AT ME."

Mamma puts her papers in her tote and searches around the floor of her study. Well, this is not strictly her study. It is also the laundry room. Mamma likes to give people the impression she does a lot of housework. The truth is, we all take turns on the laundry. But in our town a lot of women don't work, so Mamma has various defensive tactics.

She picks up a stray sock and throws it into the washing machine without looking.

"Mamma! Stop swinging your booty around and look at me. Please."

"*Booty.* I like that word."

"I know you do. Dad says it. It's part of his phony hip-hop thing. Will you please look at me?"

Mamma turns to me with a harried smile. She teaches at the local college and her classes start today, too. Her smile goes slack. "What did you do to your lips?"

So it's not a delusion. Well, at least I'm not crazy. "Nothing."

"You must have done something. Look at them. They're white."

"God hates me."

"Very funny. Did you eat ice? Or hit them hard? Or—"

"I didn't do anything."

Mamma comes over and feels my forehead. She touches my lips gently. She tilts her head—a baffled expression on her face—and I can see her eyes fighting to hold back worry. That's all it takes—now I'm really worried. Before this was just something odd—but now . . . My throat squeezes shut so hard, I can't swallow. Her hands cup to hug my cheeks, like they did when I was little and I'd get hurt. If she gets any more tender I will lose it and blubber all over.

I step away. "Am I sick?"

"Do you feel sick?"

"No."

She blinks. "Everything's normal?"

"Normal?" I point at my lips.

"Besides that."

"Yeah, right. Besides that, how was the play, Mrs. Lincoln?"

"All right, Pina, there's no point getting mad at me. I'll call Dr. Ratner. Are you ready for the bus?"

I point at my lips again.

"Besides that."

I throw my hands up in exasperation and go in to breakfast.

Mamma follows me. "Don't say a word," she says to Dad. "And, you . . ." She points as Dante comes into the kitchen. "You are to eat in silence."

Dad looks at Mamma in surprise. Then he looks at me. His lips part. He blinks. "What happened?"

"Your lips are white," says Dante.

"I mean it," says Mamma. "Silence. Besides, there's nothing to talk about until we know more." She picks up the phone and goes into the other room.

Dad cuts the pancake into quarters and puts a piece on each of our plates. We dig in.

If there's one thing in life you can count on, it's Dutch pancake. With lemon and confectioners' sugar. If I had wanted Dad to make me comfort food, this is exactly what I would have asked for. The dense, reassuring texture as my fork goes through it, the rich, egg-y smell as it approaches my mouth, and now, at last, the heavenly taste. At this moment, nothing else matters.

I love food. I love eating. I'm not fat, which I suppose is unfair, or that's what some of my friends say. When they moan about their weight, I keep quiet. I don't know why I'm not fat. I don't do sports. But I dance. I do jazz. Maybe that's the answer. Except even the girls who are major athletes complain about their weight.

The phone rings. Once. I thought Mamma was on the phone. Oh, yeah, it's only 7 a.m. Dr. Ratner's office isn't even open. The answering service must have paged him, and that's him calling back now. Mamma clearly picked it up on the first ring.

I know this routine. We are not a particularly accident-prone family. But somehow the accidents we have take place after-hours, so Dr. Ratner's always getting paged and calling us back.

Dad takes another pancake out of the oven. "Who needs seconds?" He sneaks a look at my mouth as he serves. My father would like to be discreet. The trouble is, he can never remember what's supposed to be private. You don't tell Dad a secret unless you want the whole family to know.

Dante, on the other hand, doesn't even try. He's still staring at me.

I stare right back.

"It's an okay look for eleventh grade," he says, and shrugs.

I almost gasp. He's actually trying to be nice. I could try back. "Ninth grade is good." I stop, remembering those days, how it really was.

Dante holds his fork mid-bite. "You stopped talking after one sentence. You never stop talking after one sentence. That's scary."

"Well, ninth grade is actually no good at all. You're the youngest in the school and some of the upper class jerks treat you like scum. You don't know the building—and the high school building is like a maze—so the first week you get lost all the time and wind up late for all your classes. You think you know all about studying from middle school, but you find out you've got no decent study habits at all and the grades on your first few assignments knock you flat. The teachers—"

"Stop!" Dante puts up his hands in surrender. "I liked you better when you sat there scowling with your white lips."

"You're not supposed to mention that," says Dad.

Dad's right. But I feel bad, too, 'cause I said all that stuff on Dante's first day of high school. Everything I said is true—but he didn't need to hear it all at once. I cut a large hunk off my second piece of pancake and slide it onto Dante's plate.

He eats it fast. So fast I bet he can't even taste it. And I would have savored every bite.

"Aren't you going to say thanks, at least?"

"I wanted to finish it first, before you could change your mind." He licks the corners of his mouth and smiles. "Thanks."

Mamma comes in. "Dr. Ratner said this is not an emergency. He'll call us back as soon as he gets into the office and can look at his schedule." She hesitates. "At 8:30."

"School starts at 7:30."

"Dr. Ratner is convinced this is not an emergency, Pina. If you were vomiting or bleeding or running a high fever or . . ."

"Okay, I get the picture. Looking like a freak isn't bad enough."

"He said, whatever it is, and it might be nothing, a little delay isn't going to change it."

"All right. I'll wait."

"I'll make you the earliest appointment possible. But . . ." She hesitates again; she does that when she's about to deliver bad news. She's so easy to read, I could scream. I think of pinching her. "There are no openings today. Or tomorrow. He was sure of that. The earliest he can fit you in is Thursday."

"I'll die before Thursday."

"He said you are in no danger of dying."

"Your face said I was."

"That's not true, Pina. I just worry—you know how I am. Your lips might even turn normal again by Thursday."

"Really? Did Dr. Ratner say that?"

"Something like that."

"Yeah, right. Then I'm staying home till they do."

"You're going to school."

"How can I go to school like this?"

"I have some old lipstick."

"You do?" Dad looks at Mamma as though she's a stranger.

That lipstick is probably nine hundred years old. Mamma doesn't wear lipstick. Mamma doesn't color her hair. I don't even think she owns a brush. It embarrassed me all through middle school. But I'm over that now. Besides, I don't really like makeup. It's just asking for acne. "Forget it. I have lipstick of my own."

"You do?" Now Dad looks at me as though I'm the stranger. Then he serves Mamma a second piece of pancake, though she hasn't touched the first, and sits down to his own plate, which he's already half eaten, stealing bites between pouring juice and milk and coffee for everyone. He eats with gusto. I think Dad enjoys eating as much as I do.

"I thought you were like Mom," Dante says to me with a snarky smile.

I send the smile right back, though I don't know what he's talking about. I'll deal with him—but I turn to Mamma first. "How come you let Dante call you Mom, but you burst into tears if I don't say Mamma?"

"He's a boy," says Mamma.

"That is such a bad answer. No one talks about boys versus girls that way anymore." I turn again and glare at Dante. "She's Neanderthal. How dare you say I'm like her? I'm nothing like her."

"I just meant the lipstick. I thought you hated fake stuff. You know, ugly is real—that sort of thing."

"Can it, Squirt." He is all wrong. I am not into ugly. I'm just sick of acne. And I am not like Mamma. I want to kick Dante under the table.

And minutes ago I wanted to pinch Mamma.

Do white lips turn you violent?

"HEY, SEP. LIPSTICK? At school?" Devin's waiting at the end of the walk as I come out.

"Eleventh grade—I mean, we knew that, but now it's real. Today. You ready?" These are dumb things to say, but I've got to throw her off. Talking about my lips when I don't even know what's going on will just make me nervous. Like Mamma. What's the point of making a big deal out of something that could be nothing?

"And shiny pink?"

This is all I have left from when I was ten and couldn't wait to wear lipstick. What did I do with the big stash of lip and eye junk I accumulated in middle school? Some of it was half decent. I keep my voice light. "It's the most important year. SATs count now. And all that stuff."

Devin nods. "Shiny pink is kind of cool, in like a retro sort of way."

I might jab her in the ribs with my elbow if she keeps this up. "I hear the teachers really crack down on grades this year."

"It looks good. Really. It's kind of fun to dress up for school. I mean, lots of the other crowds do it, why shouldn't we?"

"Are you even listening to me?"

"Are you listening to me?"

"How many years have we been best friends, Devin?"

"Since second grade."

"So zip it about my lipstick, okay?"

"Sure, cool. Don't get touchy." She straightens the front of her shirt. "Amanda got a bra yesterday."

Amanda is Devin's little sister. "She's twelve. No big surprise there."

"You know what she said to me when she got home with Mom? She said, 'I've been waiting for this my whole life.'"

I laugh. "Amanda's always been direct."

"I've been waiting my whole life, too."

I blink. Devin is ample in the breast area. "What are you talking about?"

"Falling in love."

I gulp. "We're sixteen. There's time."

"How do you know?"

I think about all the stuff we read last year in social studies, when Mr. Hannahs did the unit on global concerns, and all the walking-home conversations I had with Owen about doomsday worries. "Okay, there's population explosion and depletion of fossil fuels and global warming, the skies are graying, the seas are rising. But you're not a polar bear who can't find an ice floe to rest on. And you're not a Bangladeshi, whose city is about to be swallowed up by the sea. You've got time to fall in love. Plenty of it." I take a breath.

"Stop! That doesn't help." Devin pulls on her fingers and looks down. "I'm sick of being just me. No one notices me. And I'm ready for a boyfriend." Devin's voice wavers a little.

I move closer to her for moral support. "It'll happen."

"Will it, Sep? I don't mean is it likely. I'm not talking about just any sixteen-year-old girl and the likelihood of her finding true love. I'm talking about me. I'm talking about Amanda and her bra and her getting what she's been waiting for all along. For years, I've been watching everyone hook up, even back in eighth grade and more in ninth grade and almost everyone else but us in tenth grade. And I'm still waiting."

I loop my arm through her elbow so we're walking along Italian style, like I do with Mamma, and I pull her close so our sides would be touching if our arms weren't in the way. I squeeze so tight I'm practically lifting her toward me. "It will happen, Devin. Maybe not this year. Maybe not next. But it will. Soon."

"How can you be so sure?"

"You're lovable, Devin. And you're loving. It'll happen."

Devin sniffs and I realize she was on the verge of tears. "You're the best friend ever, Sep."

"So are you." And that's the truth. I love Devin. I want her to be happy. For her sake I even hope she'll fall in love this year.

"What have you been waiting for?" she asks quietly.

"You mean my whole life? Nothing."

"Come on, Sep, tell me."

"No, really. I guess I'm just not like that."

"Trust me, you are. I bet everyone is. They have to be. And I bet something good will happen to you because you look good. You look like a good person, I mean. People can see it in you. So tell me: what have you been waiting for?"

I look like a good person. What a daft thing to say. But I don't want to argue with Devin—not now, not the way she's feeling. "I'm just moving ahead, eyes open. Whatever happens, happens."

She laughs. "Right. What about the index cards?"

Devin's no one's fool. Yesterday she went with me on my annual trek to put index cards in all my new teachers' school mailboxes, asking them to please call me Sep and never use my full name in class. So she's right, I do try to control some things—but you'd have to be an idiot not to try to control something like that. "You win."

But I still don't think I've been waiting my whole life for something. I'm doing what I want to do—daily life is fine. Sure, I want to fall in love. Deep and true. But I'm not in a rush. Devin might be ready. But I'm not.

"Okay, don't tell me if you don't want to." Devin drops my arm. "Becca's having a party on Friday. Leave it to her to have the first party of the year. A dance party, of course. What are you going to wear? I bought some of those new pants, you know, the cropped ones. Everyone's got them. I was nice and took Amanda shopping last week and saw them and couldn't resist. But they look stupid on me. They make my thighs seem huge. Like a whale. Like I shouldn't walk on the Atlantic City boardwalk or some passing Japanese guy might harpoon me."

I have no idea what pants she's talking about—I've never been super observant about clothes—but she's looking at me as though she expects a reaction. "Whales don't have thighs."

"You're supposed to laugh anyway, Sep. It's called being polite."

"Sorry. Your thighs are great, by the way."

"No they're not. Whatever. I bought white, which is extra stupid, especially since I want to look juicy for this party."

That's the way the two of us have always divided the world: everything and everyone is either juicy or juiceless. We tell each other we are definitely juicy, even if no one else has noticed yet. Devin goes on and on, speed talking as though she doesn't want to give me the chance to interrupt. Right now, though, it's just fine with me to listen. My lips need time off.

They feel weird. Not because they're white. They are weird because they're white. But they feel weird because this lipstick is like a coat of car wax. Gummy. I don't remember lipstick feeling like this in middle school. Maybe old lipstick rots? What a dumb idea it was to put it on. Now everyone will react like Devin. That's the last thing I need.

Unless they act like Mamma—the worry in her eyes. That would be worse.

4

WE GET TO SCHOOL and Devin goes her way and I go mine. I put my backpack away in my locker and watch the girl beside me check her teeth in her iPod mirror. We're not supposed to bring iPods to school, but she's packing. I'm not. So I duck into the bathroom for a quick peek at the mirror—yup, ugly pink goop still there—and go to my first class, trying to act natural and disappear at the same time, which I guess sort of works, except maybe nine hundred people say hi to me, so I have to at least nod.

I don't see Dante anywhere. Probably he's already lost. I almost feel sorry for him.

Faces parade past. Some have lipstick—but not many.

And no one has pink. I bet everyone who passes is thinking, *Pink lipstick, what's up with her?* I bend my neck and look at the floor, which is clean—I bet that won't last a day. It's a pattern of dark gray diamonds with light gray diamonds in the spaces between. Ugly. I feel sorry for it.

My first class is AP Biology. I have been fascinated by animals for as long as I can remember, so I walk in hopeful, ready to get lost in the whirl of information that's sure to come.

Mr. Dupris says that swifts stop flying just long enough to nest—but that's all—the rest of the time, they are in the air.

Swifts sleep in the air.

Could that be true?

Mr. Dupris is an odd duck. According to his own outline of the semester, he's supposed to be talking about basic chemistry—water and carbon and all that. Instead, he's jumped ahead to metabolism. His eyes shine and he bounces on his metatarsals, clicking his heels each time, like a metronome. It's like he can't stop himself. Like he's the one with a metabolism problem. But I like teachers who get off the topic. They tend to talk about what they love, and that means they know details that aren't in the book.

Next is English, and it's pretty much what I expected it to be. We read a poem—that's the part of English I've always loved, the reading. And sometimes the writing. It's the discussion that bores me. Today's discussion feels aimless, like always, and my thoughts keep going back to my lips. I can't wait for this class to end.

I rush to the bathroom after English and check my lipstick. I rushed here after Bio, too. If anyone's noticed, they must think I have a urinary tract infection. Or a weak bladder. Or irritable bladder syndrome. Or I'm pregnant. And high school is a rumor mill. This is not cool. On the other hand, I can't imagine who would notice. Devin says no one notices her. But really I'm the one no one notices.

Just to be sure, though, I lock my eyes on the floor as I exit the bathroom, then race to the lunchroom that way. Today's lunch is a thick slice of spinach pie. The Italian kind. Mamma made it. It has the flakiest crust in the world, like a little miracle—it's actually worth reeking of parmigiano afterward.

"Sep? Right?"

I look up.

"I'm Rachel. We're in Bio together." She sits beside me on the bench. She's little and neat, almost prim.

"Nice to meet you."

"That has a great aroma."

I laugh. "You could smell my mother's spinach pie just walking past me?"

"I'm trying to develop a nose. Like they say in wine tasting." She looks at the pie. And not in a casual way.

It is a particularly big slice. Why not? "Want a bite?"

"Oh, could I? Thanks." She pulls a fork out of her pocket.

"You come prepared."

"You never know what you'll find." She takes a bite. "That's insanely good. Simple, but right. Spinach, onions, eggs, parmigiano, ricotta, and nothing but salt and pepper."

"Exactly. I'm impressed."

"Thanks so much. Give your mother my compliments. See you in Bio," she says as she leaves.

I finish the pie with even more appreciation than before, if that's possible. Simple, but right. You bet. Then I eat a peach from our tree, which is sweeter and juicier than anything store-bought. I finish it off slowly with a thermos of milk.

Oh no. Lipstick came off on the thermos lip. Okay. I'll go to the bathroom and touch up. No biggie. But my head goes hot anyway. I hold the thermos in front of my mouth and keep my head down and make a dash for it.

And I crash into someone.

"Sep? How you doing?"

I tip my head up. It's Joshua Winer. Oh my God. With all that curly hair. He's big. He looks like a football player, which is a stupid thought because he is a football player. I feel suddenly small. I swallow. "Fine."

"You know, I was wondering about you just the other day."

He was? I don't think we've spoken since fifth grade. But we have a history, actually. We were friends that year, fifth grade. The very first week of school Mrs. Sutton taught us all about adventure novels and put us in pairs to write survival stories. Joshua and I were paired together. We hit it off, and after that we chose each other for anything that required a partner. He was my best friend in fifth grade, except for Devin, of course—but Devin wasn't in my class that year. Then middle school came, and boys and girls couldn't be just friends anymore. If you talked to a guy, you were going with him. I couldn't even walk home with Owen, it got so bad. And Joshua got popular and I didn't. So we stopped talking. For a while I thought about him as Mr. Cool. Then I just stopped thinking about him altogether.

He smiles. "What's with the thermos?"

Good grief, I'm still holding it in front of my mouth. How much lipstick is gone? It can't be that much, right? I lower the thermos. "Nothing."

He nods affably. "So how're your classes?"

"I only had Bio and English so far." God, can he smell the parmigiano? I shut my mouth tight.

"AP, huh? Both of them?"

"Just Bio. I've never been that good at English."

"But you're good at everything else. So, did you have a good summer?"

I nod.

"I heard there's something going on at Becca's on Friday."

I nod.

"You going?"

I nod.

"So maybe I'll see you there." He smiles and waves and walks on.

I'm staring after him. No, I'm not allowed to do that—that is totally unacceptable behavior, loser behavior—no, bad girl! I look down.

Joshua Winer talked to me. Mr. Cool. And all I could do was gape. There are nine hundred things I could have said. I mean, I know the guy. He's just Joshua. How much could he have changed since fifth grade, after all? Well, a lot. But some things don't change. I could have asked how his big sisters are. We could have complained about our siblings, like we used to do.

I am not a person who counts on luck. But, hey, I deserve better luck than this. I am a great talker. Usually. Please let him remember that.

I go to the bathroom. Only a few hints of white show

near the corners of my mouth. I reapply this sticky pink.

Then I stop in the library and check Google. Mr. Dupris is not a big fat liar: swifts eat and mate and sleep in the air.

Life on the wing.

It sounds hard. And dangerous. If you're asleep, you could fly right into a cat or an owl, mouths open wide. You could fly into the trunk of a tree and brain yourself and fall dead on the ground. And with all the windmills that are going up now, ugh, you could be sliced to smithereens. If I were a swift, I'd probably become an insomniac.

Life shouldn't be like that. Everyone should have a chance to act smart and avoid dangers—so then if you don't, well, it's your own fault.

But maybe that's the point. Maybe Mr. Dupris is telling us life is like that—it isn't a matter of should or shouldn't. We can't count on fair. Some of us wind up with white lips, after all.

5

I SUPPOSE DRUGSTORE LIPSTICK is cheaper. And I'm usually thrifty. So I don't really know why I'm in this department store. Maybe I'm pampering myself. I feel the blues coming on.

That's dumb. I can't really be worried. Dr. Ratner isn't a moron. If this was serious, he would have made me come in right away instead of waiting till Thursday.

But just to be sure, I stopped back in the library after school and Googled "white lips." Sites came up about little white bumps on your lips. Herpes. My lips are smooth. Besides, there's no way I could have herpes. You get herpes from kissing someone who has it. I haven't kissed anyone since Raul last spring—and that hardly counted, and, anyway, I would have shown symptoms long before now if he'd been infected.

I think.

Another site was in Chinese. So much for that. Another site was about musical taste, and suggestions for what to listen to. Nope. Then there were sites about CO_2 training. I don't know what that is, but it can't be relevant.

So I gave up. If white lips are a symptom of something, it's probably not anything dangerous, or those things would have come up at the very head of the list. Right?

My job is to cover up and forget about it till Thursday. Easy. Sure. Like not thinking of an elephant when people say, "Don't think of an elephant."

Whatever. I'm anxious. But maybe the real reason I'm pampering myself, the real source of my impending gloom, is Joshua Winer. I want him to like me. That is a terrible realization. Our friendship in elementary school was sort of like a crush. We never kissed, of course, or even held hands. But it was special in that preteen boy-girl way. Maybe I never got over it.

I swallow. Could I be that dumb? I'm a realistic person. When groups formed in middle school, the social hierarchy quickly became clear. I'm not popular or pretty—so I'm not on Mr. Cool's tier. People from different tiers don't mix.

And that means I don't like the fact that I can't get him out of my head now.

I need a picker-upper, all right.

I have set my sights on lipstick. After all, lipstick saved the day today. Lipstick is the best short-term solution. And shiny pink, while it seemed pretty to me when I was ten, is totally ridiculous now. So here I stand, at the cosmetics counter in this fancy department store, looking at shades.

"Can I help you?" The clerk has very black, very dyed hair. Her lips are purple. She's young, and both hair and lips look good on her. Slinky, that's a name to fit her.

"Do you have lip color?"

"This is a cosmetics counter; we have lots of lipstick."

"I mean lipstick in lip color—the color of lips."

"Oh, you mean clear? You want lip gloss, then."

"No, not clear. I mean the natural color of lips."

"Everybody's got different colored lips."

"I want my color."

"What's your color?"

I was hoping she could tell from the rest of me. Oh, dear. I'm trying to remember. It isn't actually that easy. It's not like you list it on forms all the time, after color of hair and color of eyes. I know it's darker than my cheeks. "Brown."

"You want brown lipstick?" She makes it sound as though I'm demented.

"I just want to look natural."

"Then don't wear lipstick."

"Do you want to sell me lipstick or not?"

"I don't care. I get paid by the hour. What, did you think this was a commission job?"

Attitude. Everyone has attitude. I'm used to it. High school is the definition of *attitude*. But right now it makes me feel defeated. "I need help," I say, and my voice sounds pathetic even to me.

Slinky softens. She puts her elbows on the counter, rests her chin in her palms, and studies my face. "Did you choose that pink you're wearing?"

"Yes. But I was only ten then."

"Good. Do you want me to choose a shade for you?"

"Yes. Please." Then I add, "Thank you."

Her fingers run over the dozens of glossy tubes. "Here."

"That's purple."

"It's burgundy. A wine color. It's more sophisticated than that cotton-candy pink. It'll look good on you. Give me your hand."

I stretch my hand out.

She draws a heart on the back of my hand in purple lipstick. "See? Isn't that nice?"

"I'll take it."

"Apply it lightly. Not gobbed on like that."

My lipstick is gobbed on? "Lightly does it," I say.

"Do you want mascara, too?"

"No."

"Yeah, you don't really need it, with those black lashes. How about some tweezers?" She's eyeing my brows.

Does she want to totally remake me? But this is her job —right. "Tweezing hurts." I remember well from middle school.

"What's a little pain for beauty?"

"It just grows back anyway."

Slinky laughs, but in the nicest way.

I pay and half-run all the way home. Purple lipstick. What did I just do? Do I even like purple? I feel a strong need for the privacy of my bedroom. I sneak in the front door.

"Slut's home."

"Don't call her that." Mamma comes running out to me. "Why are you so late? How are you feeling?"

"No vomiting. No fever. What else did you ask this morning? Oh yeah, no bleeding."

"Unless you count her period," yells Dante from the living room.

I don't have my period. But it's coming. I can feel it in the heavy blumpiness of my belly. How did Dante know?

I stand in the hall and look at Dante. He's on the floor in front of Nonno's chair. Nonno was Mamma's father. He's been dead over a year. Still, no one sits in the soft fake leather that used to hold his indentation.

Except Rattle. Who isn't there now.

When Mamma's cooking, Rattle's in the kitchen—and Mamma's clearly been cooking. Her hands are garlic. Rattle is undoubtedly under the table, nose lifted hopefully toward the stove, since his sense of smell is great, even if he's too blind to see anything.

Rattle came from the SPCA when he was only a year old. An overgrown mutt puppy with a broken tail. He thumps it on the floor, and immediately you know it's separate pieces inside. Without all that hair, it would rattle. But there is all that hair. So how did Dante know enough to name him that, and when he was only five?

Does my brother have unknown powers?

Mamma's been looking me over this whole while. "You seem healthy. Go wash off that lipstick and let's take a peek." She clasps her hands in front of her waist.

I should tell her about the lipstick coming off at lunch and the little wispy white spots that showed. But I can't bring myself to, her face is so hopeful. And now I'm suddenly mad at her. I managed to keep a good perspective all day long and now she's ruined it. "You're making this into some big thing!"

"Me? No, I'm not." Her face falls.

She's hurt? This is so unfair. I'm the one with the white lips. "Forget it. Soap and water?"

"Cold cream. I have some."

We go to the bathroom off her and Dad's bedroom. She opens a cold cream jar. I dip in a finger and smear it over my lips. White everywhere. Then I wipe with a tissue.

The pink is gone.

My lips are white.

"It must be a character flaw," I say. "Probably fatal."

"Dr. Ratner said—"

"I was kidding, Mamma." Permanently disfiguring. Not fatal.

6

THE GRAPH OF $Y=X^2$ is a nice deep bowl of a curve with the lowest point at the origin. The sides are mirror images of each other—symmetrical. All these graphs on our calculus homework are familiar to me from ninth-grade geometry, but they're fun to do again. Symmetries galore.

I touch my lips. They are symmetrical across a vertical axis. Symmetry is part of beauty. Experiments prove that; when presented with pictures of faces, people invariably find the symmetrical ones most attractive. I read about that in sixth grade, for a school project on birds.

Animals turn out to care about symmetry, too. Female zebra finches choose mates with symmetrically colored leg bands. And beauty has a halo effect: attractive people are also judged to be more intelligent and better-adjusted. They're more popular.

So beauty matters. At least in most people's eyes. Undoubtedly in Joshua Winer's eyes.

I'm getting blue again.

None of that—back to graphs.

I like asymptotes. I don't remember if we learned that word in ninth grade. If we did, we didn't make a big deal out of it. But Ms. Brame made a big deal out of it today in class.

An asymptote is a line which a curve moves toward as it tends toward infinity but will never reach. I like that idea, though I guess it could be thought of as sad—a poor curve striving to meet a line.

I'm graphing our homework functions while I watch TV. Some CSI thing. My laptop is open beside me. I'm not doing anything with it—Devin and I already IM-ed each other. But it's just good to be logged on. Ready.

"Pina, phone," Mamma calls from the kitchen.

I heard it ring, but I never figured it would be for me. A friend would text me. So I'm jangly now. And I don't like it that whoever is on that phone heard Mamma call me Pina. I run up the basement steps and take the receiver from her. "Hello?"

"Oh, hello, it's Mrs. Harrison."

"Hi."

She wants me to babysit. I love Sarah, her daughter, but I feel suddenly tired. The last time I sat for Sarah, she painted her face with chocolate. Only it wasn't chocolate. She just thought it was chocolate. It was some kind of chocolate-flavored laxative. And she kept licking it off her hands and I didn't know how much she had eaten, so I had to call Mamma and we gave her ipecac and she vomited the rest of the night. And had diarrhea, as well. That was a normal night for Sarah.

"How was your first day of school?"

"Fine, thanks."

"I was wondering if you could babysit Friday night. We're going out around seven, and I guess we'll be back by midnight."

"I'm sorry. I can't."

"Oh." Silence for a moment. "Well, you know, you're in eleventh grade now and you have so much experience sitting, we've decided to raise your pay an extra dollar an hour. How does that sound?"

"That's nice. But I can't, Mrs. Harrison."

"Did I say 'dollar'? I meant two dollars."

"I'm already doing something Friday."

"You have a date?" She's not good at hiding her surprise.

I'm almost insulted. Except the people I'm friends with don't usually date. We hang out together. It's different. "A party. Anyway, I'm busy."

"How about a bonus of five dollars at the end of the evening? That's on top of the raise."

"It's not the money, Mrs. Harrison."

"Please, Pina."

Whining is unfair. And it's horrible that she calls me Pina. I hope that's not her new name for me. "I really can't. You'll find someone else."

"Of course. Of course I will. Good-bye." Her voice is so sad. "Enjoy your party. Good night, dear."

I hang up.

Mrs. Harrison called me dear, but she must want to kill me now. Or maybe she wants to kill Sarah.

I go back down into the basement. There's a message for me on my cell. I blink in disbelief: it's Joshua Winer.

I've texted with Joshua Winer only once before, in fifth grade. We did it just to figure out how texting worked. This feels different. Well, it is different. I stare at his question:

"hey, Sep. hows homework?"

I type: "fine." That's lame. That's what I always say. I delete and type: "normal."

"what r u doing?"

I type: "learning about asymptotes." Then I look at it. What if he doesn't know the word? I delete. I type: "not much."

"im reading physics."

I type: "i have physics next semester."

"2 bad. U could have coached me."

What do I say to that? I type: "Ha." But what if he thinks I'm laughing at him? Even when we were little, he didn't like science so much. Except the part on weather. I remember him getting all excited about precipitation and air pressure and wind and everything. He was cute. I delete and type: "i have to translate a ton of Latin."

"u should take Spanish. its easy."

I type: "MayB next semester."

"then i can coach u."

I swallow. I type: "that would B fine." Then I delete fine and type nice.

"i liked ur lipstick today."

I remember the clerk in the department store. I type: "u didnt think it looked like candy?"

"i like candy. it tastes good."

Oh . . . my . . . God. Joshua Winer is flirting with me. And he's bad at it. My cheeks are so hot, it feels like a fever. I type: "have to finish my homework. see u."

"at the party friday. gnite."

I lower myself to the floor and lie on my back and stare at the pipes that run across our basement ceiling. I close my eyes.

Yes, it is quite clear that my luck sucks: a popular guy notices me just when my lips have turned white and who knows what's wrong with me. And this particular popular guy is the grown-up version of a guy I used to know well, a guy I used to really like. And he liked my lipstick. A lot. He likes a façade that isn't me at all. Maybe he doesn't remember the me I was in fifth grade. Maybe he can't see the real me past the lipstick. Maybe once my lips turn back to whatever color they really are, and I stop with the lipstick, he'll walk off without another glance.

"What's the matter, Slut?"

"I'm dead. That's why my lips are white. All the blood has drained out of me."

"Don't joke around."

I open my eyes.

Dante's on his knees beside me. His face is actually concerned. And this morning he was nice to me. Is the whole world changing?

"I just decided to lie down."

Dante sits on the couch. "That what eleventh grade does to you?"

"How was your first day of high school?"

"You heard at dinner."

"Yeah, but that was the version you told the parents. How was it really?"

"I only got lost once."

"Good."

"I only got punched once."

"Excellent."

"I don't think Ms. LeHiste is as bad an English teacher as you said."

"To each his own."

Dante picks up my cell. "Looks like you have a boyfriend."

I jump up and grab it. There's a message—but it's just from Owen. "That's Owen, idiot."

"He's a guy."

"Guys and girls are friends in high school. Start texting girls. You'll see. It's a lot better than the stupid stuff that happens in middle school."

"Oh yeah? Friends? Look at his message."

I look at it again. Owen wrote: "the answer to sex this year."

"There's a nonromantic explanation for it, I assure you," I say.

"Like what?"

"I don't know. I haven't asked him yet."

"Yeah," says Dante, knowingly.

"Come off it. It's just Owen, idiot."

"Sure. That's how it starts. With Owen Idiot. Then he becomes Owen Not So Dumb. Then Owen Smart. Then you're in love."

"Good night, Squirt." I take my computer and cell and go upstairs.

"Good night, Slut," he calls up after me.

I go into my bedroom, close the door, drape myself across the bed, and type: "whats the answer to sex?"

"Yes, please."

Yes, please. I grin at the words. This is infantile. But I like it anyway. I type: "ur the best." And he is; he never fails to make me laugh.

I already filled out all the school registration information and cards they handed out in homeroom today. In pen. Too bad. I hate to be messy. But sometimes you have to make concessions.

I take all the forms and cards out of my backpack and search for the 'sex' slots. They usually come right after 'name.' I cross out F and write yes, but there isn't enough room to add please. Owen must have said that just for my benefit. It sounds better.

Poor Mr. Eberly. I wonder if he gets a headache or if he

just thinks we're all pathetic or if he actually laughs now and then. I would never want to be head counselor at a high school. Kids can be jerks. I'm being a jerk.

When I look back at the cell, Owen's words greet me: "so r u"

I type: "Latin then bed. see u tomorrow." I sit up and translate Latin. Usually I like nothing better than unpacking the information in a long, Latin verb, but tonight I find myself falling asleep.

I go to the kitchen and make my lunch for tomorrow. Same as what I had today. What's the use of changing when what you have is good?

7

I HIT THE ALARM clock and run to the bathroom mirror.

My lips are still white.

Tears come in an instant.

Was it ridiculous to hope that they'd turn back to lip color overnight? They turned white overnight, after all. What's to say the whole thing couldn't reverse itself?

But it didn't. And that's that. Cover it up and forget about it.

That elephant again. Don't think, don't think, don't think.

I finish my routine, then get dressed. When I go back

to the bathroom to put on my new lipstick, Dante's in there.

I have the urge to pound on the door with the side of my fist. He'd do it to me.

But I'm better than him.

I go to my room and look in the full-length mirror inside my closet door. I open the lipstick.

I can hear Slinky in my head. I apply it lightly. This color doesn't look as good on me as it looked on her, but at least I now have colored lips.

Mamma's eyes take in my lipstick and quickly go back to the kitchen counter. "Would you like an omelet? Broccoli and Asiago?" She is not the breakfast maker. Dad is. But she's good at omelets, and she's offering my favorite. She feels sorry for me.

I can ride the pity train. "Sure, thanks." I pour a glass of milk, put it on the table, and stand beside Mamma to watch her cook.

"Is that for me?" Dante comes in, sniffs loudly, and drops into a chair.

Mamma slides the omelet onto a plate and hands it to me. I'm always surprised at the speed of omelets. They taste too good to be that fast. "I'll make you the same, Dante," she says. "Pour yourself something to drink."

"Already got that covered." Dante drinks my milk.

I keep my plate in one hand and with the other I get down another glass and fill it with milk and go to the table, both hands full.

"You didn't yell at me." Dante looks at me with a milk mustache I know he made on purpose.

"What's the use?"

"You're learning," says Dante.

"And you never learn, Squirt. So, really truly, what's the use?"

"Wait!" Dad puts down his coffee. It's in a glass. I bought him a set of four glasses for his birthday. They're double-sided, with air between the two layers, so you can see the coffee, but your hands don't get burned holding the outside. They're all Dad uses now. So the design isn't just clever, it's better. And I can tell from the dopey look Dad has whenever he uses one of those glasses that he feels loved drinking from them—loved by me.

I smile. "Wait for what?"

Dad runs to the living room. Pretty soon I hear a CD. Dad comes back in. "Louis Jordan. Listen to the song 'What's the Use of Getting Sober (When You're Gonna Get Drunk Again)' It's great. And wait till you hear 'Ain't Nobody Here But Us Chickens.'" He walks around the kitchen twitching and knocking his elbows around. I think he thinks he's dancing. And I can't tell if it's supposed to be to this song or to the song about chickens.

My father is a tall, gangly mix of Swedish and Norwegian. Mamma calls him *il mio vichingo*, which means "my Viking" in Italian. It is not a pleasant sight to watch him dance. Still, I'm grinning now. He's Daddy, after all.

I finish breakfast and race to meet Devin outside her house.

Devin looks annoyed. "You didn't answer my message."

"You wrote again? I went to bed early."

"I figured. You probably finished everything fast. Did you understand the Ovid poem?"

"It was just the first twenty lines."

"Twenty lines too many," says Devin. "What was it about?"

"The usual invocation of the gods, to help the poet tell the story. Then stuff about what it was like before there was earth and sea and sky. The big chaos."

"Yeah, I got that. But what was all that at the end? It felt like a bunch of contradictions."

"It was. Cold and hot, wet and dry, soft and hard. The world was a mess in the beginning. Or that's what Ovid thought."

Devin frowns. "Latin III is going to be boring. Maybe I'll drop it."

Latin III is the only class we have together. And it's the first time we've had a class together since we started high school.

"Come on, Devin, don't drop. We can struggle through it together."

"I read on the Internet that Ovid would be fun. He's known for his erotic poems. We could use erotic poems. But there goes Mrs. Reynolds, picking his mythology poems, instead. The woman is juiceless."

"It'll get better."

"Spanish is easier."

I think of Joshua Winer. Juicy Mr. Cool. "We could do Spanish next semester."

"All the popular kids are in Spanish now."

"I hate to break it to you, Devin: Spanish won't make us popular."

"It could. If the popular guys liked us. If they recognized how hot we really are."

I laugh. "Sure, Devin."

"Are you saying I'm not hot?" She pretends to be insulted.

Devin has long strawberry blond hair, thick and wavy. She's fleshy, but in a good way, and, no matter what she says, she knows how to dress to make the best of it. Her skin is clear—I don't think she ever breaks out, even when she gets her period. She has great teeth, icy blue eyes, a nice nose. I've always known it, but never quite so clearly; I'm stunned. "You're beautiful, Devin."

"Don't say that."

"I mean it. Any guy could like you. But no one would notice me."

"What do you mean? You're totally juicy. And it really could happen, 'cause lots of couples split up over the summer."

That's been on my mind. Last year Joshua Winer was a couple with Sharon Parker. "Like who?"

"Luke and Corina. Jed and Suzanne. Lots."

"Anyone else?"

"Are you fishing?"

"Why would I be fishing?"

"You just sound like you're fishing. You're not supposed to fish with friends. You're supposed to tell me."

I can't tell her about Joshua Winer. No one in their right mind would believe Joshua Winer was interested in me. Not in that way. Maybe he isn't. Probably he isn't. "Do you think I jump to conclusions?"

"Never."

"Really?"

"You're the last person in the world to jump to conclusions." She looks me over. "If I ask you a question are you going to bite off my head?"

I stare at her.

"Why are you wearing lipstick again?"

I've been waiting for the chance to tell Devin. I decided this morning, in the shower, that I need to tell her. 'Cause I really am worried now. But all at once I panic. "Did you write yes for sex?"

"The whole eleventh grade did, I think. I never saw a message pass that fast." Devin lowers her head and talks out of the side of her mouth, like we did when we were little and pretended to be detectives. "You're avoiding my question."

"Which question?"

Devin laughs. "Are you trying to get someone with that lipstick? Who?"

"I'm trying to have color in my lips."

"I noticed. Purple." Her tone is not appreciative.

"It's burgundy."

"Next thing I know, you'll be wearing all black."

"Hey, Devin. Hey, Sep." It's Becca.

And my chance to talk seriously with Devin is gone. I half want to scream. But only half.

"So," Becca says to Devin, "have you figured out what you're wearing Friday night?"

It's Wednesday. Two more days till Becca's party.

A lot can happen in two days.

Mamma made an appointment for me with Dr. Ratner for after school tomorrow. There's still time for things to turn right again.

"Huh, Sep?" Becca elbows me.

"What?"

"I asked what you're wearing to my party?"

"Lipstick."

Becca smiles. "Lipstick and nothing else? You're changing your image. It's about time."

My image is changing on its own. But I just smile.

"And you're hardly talking. That's cool. Guys don't like girls that talk all the time like you."

I rush off to my locker. Then rush to homeroom. Turn in the cards and forms with yes for sex. Then fight off the urge to check my lipstick in the girls' bathroom and rush to AP Bio.

Mr. Dupris says tunas must swim constantly and fast, or they will die.

Like swifts. But it's worse for tunas—swifts stop to nest—but tunas don't nest—they never stop, not for anything.

Do I detect a theme in Mr. Dupris's lectures? This is only the second class of the semester, but I'm pretty good at sniffing out obsessions. And this could be another little morality tale. After all, what could be more unfair than never being able to kick back and rest? My breath catches. I don't need morality tales . . . or I hope I don't. I hope my lips are nothing awful after all. And I hope all Mr. Dupris really cares about is oddities. If he does, I am almost entirely sure Bio will be my favorite class.

In English we discuss the first chapters of Zora Neale Hurston's *Their Eyes Were Watching God*. I love the opening of this book. I've never been very happy with dialogue written in dialect. But this author makes her characters speak so I hear them.

I sit at a table near a wall in the lunchroom and open that novel and read as I eat and wait for Devin.

"No more candy?"

My stomach flips. I know who it is before I look up, of course.

Joshua Winer sits beside me. "Mind if I take a seat?"

My mind has only one thought: *Is he still with Sharon?*

I put down my thermos and sit on my right hand. Today nothing will cover my mouth; I will talk no matter what.

His knee touches mine, then moves away quickly.

It wasn't intended, I'm sure. But my heart thrums like

some trapped bird and saliva gathers in the back of my throat. I think maybe I'll gag. And my nipples stiffen. I can feel them inside my bra. No one can possibly see that. Please, let no one see that.

"Hrr . . ." I clear my throat. Come on words, you're inside there. I clear my throat again. "How did the physics go?"

"Not so bad. How did the Latin go?"

"Almost good. I don't like invocations. But I like chaos."

He nods. "There's got to be something I can understand about what you just said."

I smile. "Homework was a poem about the chaos before the beginning of time—or maybe not time—maybe before the beginning of everything. Although there was cold and hot and soft and hard and things like that, which I suppose means it couldn't have been before everything. You know how creation stories are, so mixed up, because the thought of nothingness is beyond us. Like black holes and big bangs." I'm running off at the mouth and his face says so. I should just stay quiet, like Becca said. I'm not such a great talker, after all. "Sorry."

"For what?"

"Making your eyes glaze over."

"What's that, lilac?" He's looking at my lips.

"You don't know a lot about the color of flowers, do you?"

"Do you? Come on, you were never the girly-girl type with flowers in her hair."

So he remembers me—at least a little. He's sweet. "I know lilac is light. This is burgundy."

"Like the wine. Yesterday lips like candy. Today like wine. You're getting better and better."

"Are you flirting with me?" The words came out on their own.

He shrugs and stands. "See you at Becca's." He walks away at an ordinary pace, not fast like a tuna afraid to die. His shoulders don't look afraid of anything.

I swallow. My cheeks are heavy. There's a frozen lump of pain between my eyes.

I asked him if he was flirting with me. Mr. Cool. He must think I'm a total loser.

But he said that stuff about candy and wine. What was I supposed to think?

Only I shouldn't have asked, no matter what. Please someone, shoot me.

I go the library and Google again.

Most animals are heavier than the water they displace. That means if they stop swimming, they'll drift to the bottom. So they need something to keep them buoyant. For people that's lungs. For most fish that's a swim bladder.

But bonito tunas don't have swim bladders. So they have to keep swimming. And fast, or their gills won't be able to filter enough oxygen out of the water and they'll drown. Mr. Dupris scores again.

Tunas race along even in their sleep.

Images of sleeping tunas zipping toward killer whales make me woozy. Oh my God, how lucky bears and foxes and chipmunks are. They can just curl up in a lair to sleep. And I can curl up in my bed. We're all so stupidly lucky compared to tunas and swifts.

Please, let that be true. Don't let me have a tuna's luck.

8

JAZZ DANCE CLUB MEETS Wednesday after school, and I'm looking down at the soft bulge of my belly under these spandex shorts and wondering how I could have ever thought I wasn't fat. I'm disgusting. A bloated blob.

Cramps came during calculus and my period during Latin, while we were translating a poem by Ovid.

So I wrote my own poem:

So much depends
upon

a white tam-

pon.

tucked in a
zipper pocket

beside the burgundy
lipstick

No wonder I'm not in AP English. In all my years of school, no teacher has ever praised a poem of mine. Poor William Carlos Williams. There should be a law protecting poets against idiots who mimic them.

Now I'm in dance class stretching like a big blob. I remember Devin talking about feeling like a whale. Maybe all teenage girls think they're about to get harpooned.

Maybe we all want to get harpooned. If *harpooned* means something else. I flush.

We stand tall, both arms overhead, reaching high, palms facing each other. This is a yoga asana. *Asana* is the Sanskrit word for 'pose.' Ms. Martin loves yoga, and she knows maybe nothing about jazz dance. But she agreed to sponsor our club last year—and again this year, because she figures maybe she can recruit some of us to yoga.

She actually told that to Becca, who is the best dancer in the school.

Which is probably why Becca has so many parties: she likes people to watch her when she's dancing—even just party-dancing. Becca knows how juicy she is.

And which is why Ms. Martin put Becca in charge of practice sessions last year.

Whatever. Yoga is okay with me. Stretches are fun. And they make my gut feel better.

"Trapezius down, girls." Ms. Martin walks through the three rows of us. "Think of your wings. If you keep your trapezius down, your wings won't bunch up. They can spread. And you can breathe."

And I have them; I have those wings.

The girl beside me rolls her eyes. Maybe she's a ninth grader. They always put on that ultra-sophisticated act.

When Ms. Martin stops to talk to Mona, one of the better dancers, the girl leans over and whispers to me, "What's up with that? Wings!"

From nowhere comes a huge urge to rise to Ms. Martin's defense and stomp this objection to dust. Ms. Martin talks about arms as wings all the time, and I love it. I whisper back, "It's not stupid. What's stupid is pictures of angels with wings growing out of their back and arms hanging down in front. Or that mutant Warren with wings in the third X-Men movie. That's the anatomy of insects. But birds and bats have wings in place of arms. I mean, their wings are their arms, right? And human anatomy is more like bird and bat than insect. So if angels are built in the image of humans, then their arms should be wings."

The girl looks stunned. She moves over one place in our row so she's not beside me anymore.

Instantly I want to bite off my tongue. I look around to see if anyone overheard.

Becca is behind me, glaring. "I thought you were trying out a new image." She steps forward. "Really, Sep, you have to stop doing that. Lipstick and nothing else at my party will be fine. But science lectures? No. No more boring talk. That's a rule. For your own good."

I love science—things are true or false in science, it's not just all opinions that lead nowhere. Everyone should love science. But I remember Joshua Winer in the lunchroom today—how his eyes started to focus on the wall behind me.

I pay attention to Ms. Martin again. Maybe concentration will redeem me.

After we've gone through a half dozen more asanas, a girl raises her hand. She's a senior. Melanie someone. I know her from Jazz Dance Club last year. "Did you bring music?"

This question is rude, but also necessary. Ms. Martin is showing no sign of wanting to include jazz dance at all today. She looks flummoxed at the very idea of music.

"Because I did," says Melanie. "Can I put it on?" She's already walking to the tiny closet where the CD player is. There's a small yellow-and-pink tattoo on the inside of her right ankle. I stare a second, while the import of what a tattoo can do—what it can hide—sinks in.

With respect to tattoos, there are three kinds of people: people who don't have them and never will; people who might get one or already have one and might get a second or even a third, but that's all forever; and the tattooed people. The tattooed people are addicted. They have many. Or if they don't have many yet, they will and they know it.

I know this because my old friend Sola became a tattooed person in ninth grade. She moved away after eighth grade, but she e-mailed me all about it. The first time she got a tattoo, the artist said to her, "Is this your first? It won't be your last." She said she knew it was true. As of the last time she wrote, she had seven.

I've always figured I was in the first group—no tattoos ever.

Melanie takes a CD out of a backpack lying on the floor beside the closet door. Within a minute we are listening to drums, rattles, plinkity things. "Here come the drums!" Melanie shimmies her way back to her spot.

"Becca? Becca?" Ms. Martin looks around like a tuna who's been forced to halt, terrified of drifting downward into the abyss. "Oh, there you are."

Becca leads us for the rest of the hour. I like this music. It makes you have to move. Even when you're a big blumpy thing with a tampon jammed inside you.

At the end of class I go up to Melanie. "Great music. Who's it by?"

"John Hanks. 'Here Come the Drums.'" Melanie smiles.

This is what tunas need to listen to when they get discouraged and wonder what's the use. But I remember what Becca said, and I keep my mouth shut.

I check the mirror in the girls' locker room and touch up my lipstick.

By the time I get to the parking lot, the after-school activity busses have already left.

"Sadistic, huh?" It's Owen. He comes up beside me and I'm instantly happy. Owen's the best.

I raise an eyebrow at him.

"The school board members are evil. They supply busses, but the busses leave the parking lot five minutes after the hour. Activities are supposed to stop on the hour. But even if they do, with putting away athletic gear or music instruments or even just taking a whizzy, most people wind up missing the bus." He smiles. "Sadistic. Walk you home?"

Owen lives two blocks away from me. We've walked home together nine hundred times. We start out in the same instant, legs synchronized. He's only a little taller than me, so it's easy to stay in step. We've always fit this way.

I look at him. He must have had a haircut for the start of school, 'cause he looks a lot less shaggy than usual. He looks nice. I smile at him. "Were you at Chess Club?"

"Chess Club's tomorrow. Want to join?"

I shake my head. Owen's good at chess. He taught me how to play it after Nonno died and I couldn't bear to be at home because of how sad everyone was. We spent whole days together then. Not talking, just focusing on chess moves. It was a good distraction, but I never really came to like the game much.

"Starting a jellyfish club?"

I blink. "What?"

He taps his bottom lip. "Pink. Purple. What next? Blue?"

"Lay off, Owen." I shift my backpack to the other shoulder. "I wrote yes. Then again, everyone in eleventh grade did."

"Not everyone. Twenty-three people didn't."

"How do you know that?"

"Mr. Eberly made me stay after today. That's where I've been, in his office, changing yes back to M or F on everyone's emergency contact cards and health cards."

I laugh. "How did he know you started it?"

"He's not a total idiot."

I laugh again. "Did you memorize the names of the twenty-three traitors?"

"No. But I screwed them. I changed their M's to F's and F's to M's. Now all the girls will get invitations to meetings on masturbation and all the guys will get invitations to meetings on managing PMS."

"Nice."

"Unfortunately, I also probably screwed a bunch of loyalists, since I don't know everyone in eleventh grade and some of them had crossed out so heavily I couldn't read what they had written before they put in yes, so I assigned M or F randomly to people with names like Pat Baldwin or Haguchi Yamatachi."

"I love you, Owen." I can't believe how good it is just to walk and talk with him. "Do they really have meetings on masturbation and not invite the girls?"

"Ready to start a revolution, huh?"

"You're the one who plots against the powers that be, not me."

"Yeah, right—when are you going to fix that? Anyway, I was just joking. The guy meetings are mostly on not using steroids for sports. But the real crime is that they don't invite guys to the PMS meetings. I mean, come on, that should be part of our self-defense instruction."

"I take it back: I don't love you. Talk like that and you can walk home alone."

"Major threat. Okay, change of subject. How's math going?"

"Why? So you can amaze me with how much more you know?"

"Of course."

Owen took calculus last year, even though he's in the same grade as I am. He's our class's math whiz. He's really the whole high school's math whiz, because last year he scored second in the school on some national test, and the girl who scored first graduated. This year he's taking a math class at the college.

"Why don't you tell me about your college course?"

"Abstract algebra. You would love it." And off he goes, into vectors and matrices.

The funny thing is, it's great to hear. I love complex systems. I could listen to Owen forever. And he knows that. He might be the only one in the world who knew I would love this very conversation.

9

RATTLE GREETS ME BEFORE I'm even halfway to the kitchen. That dog can smell blood a mile away. His big blind head comes banging into my crotch.

I get on my knees and scratch him behind both ears at once. He loves that. "You can't do that, Rattle. Just be a good dog and I'll let you sit by my feet as I do my homework."

And that's how the evening goes, with Rattle by my feet farting in his dreams, Dante moaning over having to write an essay already and it's only the second day of school, Mamma blinking away her fear when she helps me cold-cream off the lipstick to find only white again, and

Dad belching as he reads a legal brief, which is better than farting, at least.

My cell has a message from Devin tonight, but no one else. I don't read it.

Where's Joshua?

Maybe he's already realized I'm boring, so he's stopped flirting. That is, if he was flirting with me—and for the life of me I can't figure out anything else he could have been doing. Well, it's okay if he's stopped. There was something great about flirting with him, but at the same time something awful. The last thing I need is a guy who's turned on because he likes my lipstick.

I finish my homework and am grateful to finally collapse into bed.

My eyes are closed. But I can't sleep. Tomorrow is Thursday. Tomorrow I see Dr. Ratner. It's been only two days— but these two days have dragged. Tomorrow I find out.

I pat my lips.

Slap them lightly, then harder.

A sob catches in my throat.

Rattle comes galumphing onto my bed and plops on my chest and licks me right up the face. His big tail thumps on my knees.

He sleeps in my room only when I have my period. He's like a big sign on the wall: blood here. Blood and garlic, a strange set of favorite odors. Maybe he's a self-hating vampire at heart.

I wrap my arms around him and cry.

Rattle licks my tears and my snotty nose. His fur stinks. Right now, though, I love it. I love him.

The next day I somehow make it through Bio and English. I move on automatic, as if in a haze. Not even lunch perks me up.

Devin dropped Latin III. And no one's talking to me in the lunchroom. And I have white lips.

I can't stop myself from looking around.

Where's Joshua Winer?

Why are my lips white?

I think I'm going crazy.

After school, I walk to the pike. Dr. Ratner's office is a block past the mall. Mamma said she'd meet me there late, because she's teaching an afternoon class. Fine. I don't need anyone holding my hand.

It takes forty minutes to walk to the doctor's. I'm a sweatball by the time I get there. I sign in and take a seat in the waiting room.

"Sep?"

I look up in surprise at the nurse. "It's not my appointment time yet." I have another fifteen minutes of ignorance—isn't ignorance supposed to be bliss?—don't steal them, please.

"The appointment before yours cancelled. Come on in." She smiles.

I follow her through the doorway into the inner sanctum. I have done this dozens of times. Dr. Ratner's been our family doctor since before I was born. I take off my shoes and step on the scale. Then the nurse leads me to an examining room and tells me to sit on the examination table and takes my blood pressure. She gives me a gown.

"It's just my lips."

"All right, then. Keep your clothes on. The doctor will be with you in a minute."

And he is.

"Dr. Ratner? You're never on time."

He smiles. "And I'm not today. If you were the patient who cancelled, we'd be starting fifteen minutes late. Why don't you come sit down here on this chair?"

I perch on the very edge of the chair.

He sits by the little desk and scoots his chair out to face me. "So, Sep, what's the problem?"

"My lips are white. Under this lipstick."

He opens a drawer and hands me a little foil package.

I read: *Makeup Remover.* I go to work on my lips.

Dr. Ratner hands me a small mirror.

I finish up and hand it back to him.

Dr. Ratner studies my lips. "Well, you're right. White lips." He pulls out a notebook and picks up a pen. "I'm going to ask you a lot of questions. If you give an answer and then later you want to change it, just change it. I'm fishing. And I need to know as much as possible. Don't be afraid to tell the truth."

Fishing. That's what Devin asked me if I was doing.

"I won't keep anything back. I want to know what's wrong with me."

"How's it been in the bathroom? Any blood in your stool?"

"No."

"Anything odd? Pus in your stool? Loose stools?"

I'm shaking my head.

"Anybody in your family have colitis?"

"I never heard of it."

"Crohn's Disease? Colon cancer?"

"Not that I know of." He said cancer. I feel nauseated. I think I'll vomit.

"Have you been tired lately?"

"Not especially."

"Here, let's just be sure. A little iron test, okay?" He goes to a counter and pours clear liquid into a small flask. Then he jabs my finger with a teeny tiny needle and holds the thinnest glass tube I've ever seen against the bubble of blood. The blood goes up the tube, and he puts a drop into the flask. It sinks quickly. "Good, no anemia. Lost any weight lately?"

"No."

He takes one of my arms and examines it all over. Then the other. "Stand up and hike your skirt up." He looks up and down and around both legs. "Okay, you can drop your skirt. Any lesions on your trunk?"

"Lesions?"

"Sores, spots, bruises, anything?"

"No."

"How about your joints? Any pains in your knees or shoulders or hips?"

"I just went to jazz dance yesterday. But I'm sore in my muscles, not my joints."

"How about nausea? Cramps?"

"I got my period yesterday. I had cramps. But just normal." I don't tell him I almost spewed on him when he said cancer.

He takes a little flashlight out of a drawer and shines it in my eyes. "No inflammation. All right." He puts the flashlight away. "Do you smoke?"

"No."

"And you're not obese." He looks at my chart. "Your

blood pressure is normal. And you already told me you dance, so you get regular exercise, right?"

"Right."

"Stick out your tongue."

I stick it out.

"Nothing sore?"

"No."

"Insomnia?"

"A little last night, worrying about seeing you today."

"Constipation? Flatulence? Sense of fullness?"

"Nothing beyond period junk."

"Any pain when you urinate?"

"No."

"Sit down. Trouble seeing?"

I sit. So does he. "No."

"And you don't live near a nuclear power plant," he mutters. "How much soy do you eat?"

"I like Chinese food, if that's what you mean. We have it maybe once a month."

"How about soy bean curd?"

"It's too bland."

"Do you take any medications?"

"You know I don't."

"No. I know I haven't prescribed any. But do you take any? Like lithium?"

"No."

"Do you eat a lot of raw broccoli or cabbage or kale or anything like that?"

"I'm not sure what 'anything like that' means, but we cook our vegetables. Except salad stuff. And carrots."

"Does anyone in your family have thyroid disease? Diabetes? Addison's Disease?"

"No to all of them. At least if we're talking about Dante and my parents. Beyond that, I don't know." I'm starting to feel unreal. The questions come too fast.

He palpates my throat, playing his fingers around the bump of my larynx. "Ever had an asthma attack?"

"No."

"Ever taken Prednisone or another glucocorticoid hormone?"

"I never take medications."

"Are you dizzy when you stand up?"

"Sometimes I've felt dizzy lately. Mostly when I think that maybe I'm dying."

"You're not dying, Sep."

"Promise?"

"Just about. I'll give you some tests so I can say yes for sure. But my guess is ninety-nine point nine percent sure. Do you crave salty foods?"

"I always love salty foods. But I love all foods. My mother cooks Italian."

"Are your periods irregular?"

"They're like clockwork."

"Are you irritable or depressed?"

"Irritable? You'd have to ask my family. Depressed—I think today I've been sad. I'm really afraid."

"You're not dying, I told you." But he doesn't say it's nothing. He doesn't say he's ninety-nine point nine percent sure it's nothing. "Do you have any lower back pain? Abdomen pain? Leg pain?"

"No for all."

"Okay. Here's what we'll do. One big cause of loss of pigmentation is Addison's Disease. You don't have any other symptoms of it. But we'll take a blood sample and test you anyway. Another is thyroid disease. Again, you don't have any other sign of it, but we'll do a few tests on that blood. Another is diabetes. Again, no other sign—but we'll test your blood for that, too. Then there's pernicious anemia, but I know you don't have that. Still, we'll test your blood. And there's ulcerative colitis. I'll send you home with a little packet so you can take stool samples and bring it back for us. But you don't have that, either."

"So what do I have?"

"Let's get the blood results before we discuss it at length. And I want you to do a small thing for me. Anyone in your house have dandruff?"

"Dante."

"How's he doing?"

"His lips are normal color."

Dr. Ratner smiles. "How about the rest of him. Is he okay?"

"As okay as Dante ever is."

"Does he use Selsun Blue?"

I give a half smile, this feels so weird. "Yes."

"Okay, good. Smear Selsun Blue on your lips and go sit in the sun in the backyard."

"My lips don't have dandruff."

He laughs. "There's a slight chance you have a fungus under the skin. If so, that will kill it. But don't stay out too long. I don't want you to get burned. A half hour at a maximum, okay? Just once. And I don't think it's a fungus, anyway. Let's just cover all the bases, though. And Selsun Blue is a cheaper way to rule that out than a Kott prep test."

"What do you think it is?"

"I don't like to make guesses without more information."

"But you already have. You said you don't think it's a fungus. So what do you think it is?"

He sighs through his nose and looks at me and I can tell from his eyes that this is not going to be good news.

I feel myself crumbling inside. I swallow. But I keep my eyes on his.

"It might be vitiligo."

"I never heard of it. Do you die from it?"

"I told you, you're not dying. No one dies from vitiligo. It doesn't affect your health, only your appearance."

Vitiligo. Vitiligo. Vitiligo. "What is it?"

"It's an autoimmune disease. Your immune system has made a mistake and is attacking you. In vitiligo the pigment cells get destroyed and white patches form on the skin."

"It starts at the lips?"

"It can start anywhere. Did you have a blow to your lips recently?"

"No."

"Then I don't know why it started there. Limbs often show it first. And usually the patches are irregular. You're kind of lucky that your lips are wholly white—and both of them."

There's pressure on my inner ears. Like I'm underwater. Like my eardrums are about to break. Like my head will explode. Vitiligo. Vitiligo. Vitiligo. "So now other white patches will come?"

"I don't know."

I look at him hard.

"Probably. Some people have mild cases. A few spots that appear suddenly and that's all. For other people there are more and more spots."

"So I'm turning into an albino?"

"No. It never goes that far. Your eyes won't change. It's just patches on the skin. Rarely, but sometimes, in the hair, too."

"Little patches? Like the opposite of freckles?"

"Or big ones. Your skin is dark, so it could be . . . noticeable."

"Is there a cure?"

"No. But there are some treatments that have had variable success. We can talk about them. Let me get the blood test and stool test back first. And you try the Selsun Blue. And then we'll talk. In a week."

"Can't we do it sooner?"

"The tests take time. We don't want to schedule an appointment and then not have all the information we need. Anyway, I'll send you to a dermatologist if you're going to try any of the therapies."

"Why not just send me to a dermatologist right away?"

"Let's take it one step at a time, okay, Sep?"

I'm blinking hard. "How did I get it?"

"No one knows. It's nothing you ate. Or did. Sometimes stress can make it worse, but we don't think stress causes it in the first place. Don't blame yourself. It's not your fault. It just happens."

"Who does it happen to?"

"More people than you think. I'll gather you some information on it for next week. Make an appointment after the nurse takes your blood. One vial will do for all the tests. In the meantime don't drive yourself crazy on the Internet."

"You know I will. Vitiligo, vitiligo, vitiligo."

"Yes, I know you will. But promise me you won't panic. There's things we can figure out together if it's really vitiligo." His eyes are steady. And they're sad. How often does he have to deliver bad news?

OhmyGod—this is bad news.

10

MAMMA IS WAITING FOR me as I come out of the lab room. She touches the Band-Aid on the inside of my elbow, from where they took my blood.

I make an appointment for next Thursday, with Mamma silent at my side.

We get into the car. She starts up the engine and backs out of the parking place. She's not asking me anything.

"Did you already talk to Dr. Ratner?"

She nods. "He took me aside while you were getting your blood drawn."

"Can we go to the college library and see if they have a book on it?"

Mamma glances over at me. "Good idea."

I use the little mirror on the back of the sun visor in front of the passenger seat and reapply my lipstick. And I used to think this mirror was pointless.

We spend the next hour at the library, finding nothing worth checking out. Mamma talks with a reference librarian, who tells us to try a medical school library. The closest is in Philadelphia.

We're back in the car.

"Can we stop at the mall? I need something."

"All right."

"And I want to go get it alone."

"All right. I'll pick up some boxer shorts for your brother."

"Get him something embarrassing."

"You can give him embarrassing boxers for his birthday if you want. I'm his mother. I'm getting what he likes." She pulls into a parking spot. "Meet me back here in a half hour?"

"Fifteen minutes is enough."

I walk into the department store at the east end and go straight to the cosmetics counter.

"Good. I was hoping you'd be here."

Slinky turns to me and blinks. "Hey, it's you again. That burgundy looks good."

Her smile of recognition lit her up. I didn't notice it before because of the dyed hair and black clothes and all, but she's totally juicy. "Actually, I botched it up with the pink this morning. I tried to mix them. So if you really think it looks good, it's only because you picked the color."

"So now you're a shrink?" Slinky tilts her head, almost coquettishly. "They're all certifiable—true psychos, you know. You don't seem the type."

"I want blue lipstick."

She slaps the counter. "That answers it."

"And green. Lime green."

"Green is in. But for blouses and purses. If you put green on your lips, it makes you look like you're standing under a neon light. People might stop and offer to give you blood. And even out in the sun, with your skin . . . I don't know."

"My skin is changing."

"Oh yeah? That's a good trick."

"I doubt it."

Slinky looks at me thoughtfully. "How about this moisturizing lip color?" She opens a skinny tube.

"It looks like mud."

"Brat."

I throw up my hands in mock offense. "There's no need to call me names."

"That's the name of the color. Hard to believe, huh? The company should fire their marketing division. Anyway, I picked it because last time you said you wanted brown."

"And you treated me as though I was a moron."

"I was new on the job. Now I know better. The customer is always crazy. That's our motto." Her hand searches through the merchandise. Her fingernails are purple. For an instant I think of Devin. Devin loves nail polish.

My chest goes pang. I miss Devin right now. I miss her so much. I can hardly believe I haven't told her anything— not about my lips, not about Joshua Winer. I've never kept a secret from her before. What kind of person keeps two secrets from her best friend for three whole days?

"How about this lip pencil in Cocoa Lights?" Slinky holds up the pencil. "If you use gloss and then pencil over it, it gives a sheer look."

"I hate it."

She takes a deep breath and protrudes her lips in thought. "Express tubes, that's the answer. They're lipstick and liner in one. It saves time. Here, look at these: Rush Naked, Coffee Run, and Racy Raisin."

Do I need to save time? My heart seems to flutter at the thought. I feel out of breath. "Do I look like a swift to you?"

"A swift? You mean a bird?"

"Or a tuna?"

"You mean a fish?"

"Do I look like I'm in a rush—running—racing?"

She stares at me. "Okay, let's go back to blue." Her eyes are nervous. We've been joking so far and she's been quick on the repartee. But now I can see she's afraid that this isn't just a little game—she thinks maybe I'm really psycho. "You're right," she says sweetly, "you could pull off a gray-blue. Like this lip color here. Silver Plum."

"Do you have anything in hazelnut?"

"Yes."

"Yes?" I practically shriek.

"That brings us back to brown tones, though. But here." She rolls a tube across the glass counter to me. "This one is right for you. Why do you want hazelnut?"

"It's my mother's favorite flavor. And my mother loves me."

"She's not the only one."

"How do you know that?"

"Jesus loves you."

Oh my God. I'd be offended if I wasn't so stupefied. For all she knows, I'm Buddhist or something. "And here I thought you were a classic alternative type."

"Don't judge a book by its cover."

I stare at Slinky—at her dyed black hair and purple lipstick. "How old are you?"

She smiles. "Older than you. I have a son." Her whole face softens. "Take the Hazelnut. Then come back and tell me how it worked."

"I'll take both." And I don't believe she's much older than me. A son, huh? Wow. On an impulse, I add, "And some purple nail polish, please. The color you're wearing."

"Hazelnut lipstick with purple nail polish? Crazy. But, hey, that's how we got our motto."

11

I DO MY HOMEWORK between sneaking looks at pictures of people with vitiligo on the Internet. I'm using Dad's computer—so I won't even think about IM-ing. And I put my cell in a drawer. No distractions. Vitiligo. It's awful how many pictures there are.

Some are of naked people, but none of them are erotic. Vitiligo makes you look so ugly, no one could get turned on. A lump forms in my throat, so big my ears ache. I've been telling myself vitiligo is just lack of coloring, so no matter how far it goes, it can't look that bad. But it does. I can't understand how—but it does. It's revolting. A little shiver hums inside me, elusive and eerie.

Normally, I would be ashamed of myself for thinking this way, for being such a shallow jerk. In fact, I'm pretty sure I wouldn't think this at all. Normally, I would have empathy. If it weren't me, I could look and be kind, charitable. But it is me.

My head is muck.

I'm not prepared for this.

Well, who could be?

Only I'm the girl who's always prepared. I work at it. I want to be ready for whatever's coming next. I always just assumed what was coming next was good.

But it isn't.

I can't deal with this right now. I can't deal with anything.

I go to the kitchen phone and punch out the numbers.

"Hello?" It's that high-pitched four-year-old voice I know too well. Shouldn't she be in bed by now?

"Hi, Sarah. It's Sep. How you doing?"

"I'm in trouble."

"What a surprise."

"At school."

"As good a place as any."

"Know what I did?"

"You can tell me later. Can I talk to your mother?"

"I bit Clancy."

"You're four, Sarah. Almost five. You know biting is antisocial."

"What's *antisocial* mean?"

"You can guess."

"Bad."

"Right."

"He deserved it."

"I'm sure he did. But that doesn't matter. When people are rotten, we try to help them, not bite them."

"No one helps me."

"That's not true. Besides, no one bites you, either."

"Clancy did."

"Oh." This changes things. A little. "Did you bite him back? Is that what happened?"

"No. I bit him first. He bit me back."

I stifle a laugh. "Can I talk to your mother now?"

I hear the phone clatter, probably falling to the floor.

"Hello, Sep? Is that you?"

"Do you still need a sitter for tomorrow night?"

"Yes."

"Are you still paying two dollars more an hour?"

"Yes."

"Plus a five-dollar bonus at the end of the night?"

"Yes."

"Then I'll do it."

"Thank you! Can you be here at seven?"

"Sure."

"Thank you, I'm so grateful. And you'll have plenty more parties you can go to. You'll see."

Right. "See you tomorrow, Mrs. Harrison."

I take a bath because it's easier to inspect myself in the bath than the shower. With a hand mirror, I examine every inch of my body I can possibly see.

I get out and towel off and sit on the sink with my rear to the medicine cabinet mirror and use the hand mirror to see the center of the back of my head and neck.

This is dumb.

I go to my room, clutching that hand mirror, and check myself out top to bottom in the full-length mirror inside my closet door.

There are no other white spots on me. Yet.

I fall in bed. All at once I realize I haven't called Devin. I was going to. I promised myself I was going to tell her everything. But I'm in bed now. And I feel like a heap of heavy dung. I couldn't get up if I tried. But I don't try.

My stomach burns like nothing I've ever felt before. Flames shoot up the center of my chest. I've heard about heartburn in TV commercials. I'm giving myself indigestion. I'm becoming certifiable, like Slinky said.

And I'm going to be very ugly very soon.

12

IN THE MORNING I put on the blue lip color. I'm not exactly sure what the difference is between lip color and lipstick beyond the fact that one is skinny, so you get less for your money.

Silver Plum. It isn't actually very blue. And it is actually very pretty.

Suddenly I'm furious. I don't even know why. I jam the top on the lip color so fast, I catch it wrong and break off the tip. More money wasted.

"Cool lipstick," says Devin, first thing.

"It's a disguise."

"Maybe. Or maybe you're becoming someone else."

"Have you been doing mind probes again?"

She laughs.

"I got something for you, too." I hand her the purple nail polish.

"How come?"

"Just 'cause I love you."

"Thanks. I love it." Devin puts it in her pocket. "And I love you, too. Hey, you're not going to believe this: I heard someone talking about you. In a good way."

There goes that heartburn. "Who?"

"Well, actually, I didn't hear it. Rachel did. And she told me."

I like Rachel; she loves Mamma's spinach pie. "So . . . ? Out with it. Who was talking about me?"

"Guys. They were listing girls. And your name came up. I told you it was possible. You have to learn to trust me." Devin talks. On and on.

I should interrupt her. Say I have something to tell her.

But I don't, and Becca joins us. And now it's two motor-mouths.

As we reach school, I compose my face. Casual is the rule. "Oh, Becca, I meant to tell you, I'm sorry, but I can't make it tonight."

"You're not coming?" Becca catches me by the elbow. "Really? You're not going to some other party, are you?"

"Of course not. I just can't do a party tonight."

"Did you get grounded? You! I can't believe it! What did you do?"

I'd laugh if I wasn't so sad. "Mamma's never even heard of grounding."

"Sep, you've got to stop calling your mother 'Mamma.' I've been telling you that since sixth grade."

"Yeah, right, I'm hopeless."

"Wow." Becca steps back and studies my face. "You're really upset. What happened?"

"I got to run. I hope the party's great." I hurry to my locker.

Devin's at my side. "How could you do that?"

"What?"

"How could you not tell me? I was counting on going with you. You knew that. I can't believe you did that."

"I'm sorry. It just happened. Last night."

"What? What happened?"

My throat has done that shut-trick again. It's been doing that a lot. It feels like it's closed to the size of a straw. Maybe I'll suffocate. "I can't talk now."

"You can't talk ever. I texted you last night, but you never answered. I tried Wednesday night, too. I keep telling myself you're not trying to avoid me. I keep smiling and joking with you. But now this. You just flaked out on me. Parties aren't any easier for me than for you, you know. I act excited because you're supposed to act excited. But you know how I'm really feeling. So what's the matter, Sep? You're supposed to be my best friend. What's going on?"

I have to tell her. But not here. I would rather someone stab me through the eyeball than cry in the school hall. "Drop it, okay?" I stash my backpack and grab my stuff for Bio and English.

"All right. I get it, Sep. I get this message loud and clear."

I turn, but she's disappeared in the hall crowd.

What a jerk I am.

In Bio Mr. Dupris tells us enzymes are proteins that catalyze chemical reactions. That means they speed them up. He shows us a picture of a white cat with blue eyes. He calls it an albino.

I sit up straight so fast, I smash my knees on the underside of my desk.

"Is something wrong, Sep?" Mr. Dupris looks worried.

I feel myself flush. Find something to say. Fast, girl. "I thought albinos had pink eyes."

"Most do. But in some albino cats, the eyes can be blue. This cat is missing an enzyme that would catalyze the reaction that would allow the amino acid tyrosine to produce melanin. Melanin is responsible for skin pigmentation."

So that cat is white because he's missing an enzyme. "What enzyme?" I blurt out.

"Good question, Sep. Tyrosinase." Mr. Dupris looks proud of himself. "And the enzyme that catalyzes the chemical reaction that breaks down proteins into their component amino acids is called proteinase—or protease, for short. Can you see the pattern?"

A half-wit could see the pattern. No one answers. We're not half-wits.

"You take the name of the substance that the enzyme acts on and you attach the suffix -ase, and, presto . . ." Mr. Dupris snaps his fingers. "You've got the enzyme name. It doesn't work all the time, but it comes close."

Mr. Dupris should date Mrs. Reynolds, the Latin teacher. She's always going bananas over analyzing words. But she's married. And probably thirty years older than him. Maybe forty. Still, they could be open-minded about it.

"Now look at these photos." Mr. Dupris shows two more photos. "Here's a black cat. And here's a black cat, but with some red hair right there." He taps the photo. "They're the same cat. When they changed the cat's diet so that it had very little tyrosine in it, some of his hair turned red."

Dr. Ratner said my hair wouldn't change color. Or, rather, he said it was rare—and only in patches.

But then, I'm not a cat.

I have nine hundred questions. But this class is about enzymes, not about pigmentation. That was just an example to make Mr. Dupris's point. I suck in the sides of my cheeks and try to listen. We're having an enzyme quiz on Monday.

English class is interminable. Mr. Batell has a gravelly voice that makes me think of grating off all my skin, and that idea makes me even jumpier.

I gobble my lunch as I walk. Joshua didn't come talk to me at lunch yesterday, which probably means he's moved on, and Devin sure isn't about to invite me to sit near her, so what's the point of going to the lunchroom? I go directly to the library.

Cats that are missing tyrosinase are not only albino, if they have blue eyes, they are also often deaf. And it isn't even all white cats with blue eyes—because lots of other things can cause white hair and lots of other things can cause blue eyes.

White connected to deafness.

Nothing I read said I might go deaf.

I close my eyes. Someone coughs. Someone turns a page. A chair leg scrapes the floor. Birds and people do their thing outside the window. The librarian speaks softly. The air itself seems to make noise. What's silence like? Constant silence?

I open my eyes and type again. Fast. My fingers fly. It turns out a mutation in tyrosinase is responsible for albinism in humans, too. In pretty much anything that can be albino, in fact. Even plants. But whiteness from vitiligo has nothing to do with any mutation or malfunctioning of tyrosinase.

So much for that.

Still, if I want color, I might try increasing my tyrosinase. Tyrosinase contains copper. I search around a bit. Nuts and oysters contain a lot of copper. So does organ meat—but I will never eat organs, yuck. Maybe I should learn to like oysters. And I love nuts. Especially Brazil nuts.

Only now I find articles about high levels of copper in our blood being connected to depression, bad PMS, learning disabilities, senility, and schizophrenia.

In other words, nuts make you nuts.

I'm joking. What am I doing, joking?

I lean back and pick at a spot on the base of my thumb. It's brown, not white. A hint of blood shows instantly. Rosy. On an impulse I Google "scrape off skin" and find a site about pumice stones. They are a gentle way of removing skin, especially rough, stained skin, like on feet and elbows. My lip skin is not rough and the problem is, there's no stain to remove.

I could buy a pumice stone and rub and rub and rub like a maniac, until my skin was gone and my lips bled. But they'd only scab up, and when the scab fell off, they'd be white again. Plus I hate the idea. When Devin and I were little and she wanted to be blood sisters, she pricked herself with the pin, handed it to me, and held up her bloody thumb, waiting. But I threw the pin in the trash and ran home. I couldn't mutilate myself.

I kiss the tiny hurt on my thumb.

I should have kissed everyone in the world while my lips still had color.

13

MAMMA'S WAITING FOR ME in the car as I come out of school. She beeps, but I've already seen her. She drives a baby blue VW bug, the old kind, so it's easy to spot her even when you're not looking for her. It's in mint condition, which means everyone admires it.

I get in and look down so I won't see the eyes of car aficionados. "What's up?"

"We can use the medical library at UPenn. I thought we might go now."

"Who did you have to sleep with to work that out?"

"Very funny. The husband of one of the English professors teaches there."

"I thought you hated all English professors."

"I do. But they don't know that. Besides, I only hate them when they talk. How was your day?"

I wonder if my dislike of literary-criticism talk comes from Mamma. And here I thought she hardly influenced me at all. "We learned about limits."

"Limits? Well, I should hope everyone in eleventh grade already knows about limits." She puts on a fake school-marm voice.

"This is math, Mamma. Limits are an interesting idea. You can talk about the value of something as it approaches something else. Like if you put a triangle inside a circle, with the three points touching the circle, well the triangle covers less area than the circle. But if you put a square inside the circle, it still covers less area than the circle, but more than the triangle did. And you could keep going. You know, putting in a pentagon and then a hexagon and whatever, on to an infinite number of equal-length sides. You get closer and closer to the area of the circle, but you never quite get there."

Mamma doesn't say anything.

She's like everyone else; I bore her. "You're not listening."

"I am, too. You said, 'You never quite get there.' But, you know, Pina, it sounds close enough."

I look at her surprised. Is my mother brilliant? "I bet you're right."

"Right? Me? I thought I was your mother, and that meant I'm never right."

"This time you might be. I bet we're going to be looking at cases where close is all you can get, but close is enough."

"Enough for what?"

"I don't know. We haven't gotten there yet."

She laughs, and I wasn't even trying to be funny.

We park in a parking garage. I let out a yelp. "You mean we're not going to circle the area nine hundred times to try to find a meter?"

"I thought you had a babysitting job tonight. Time is limited." She smiles. "Limits, you see."

No, I don't see. That's not the same idea at all. My mother is not brilliant. Well, that's a relief. She's pretty—at least I can be the smart one.

We go through many doors and Mamma explains to three librarians, each one more important than the last, before the name of Professor Diaz makes magic happen. The fact that Diaz is his last name explains why Mamma can talk to his wife, the English professor. Mamma can overlook a lot about people if they speak a Romance language.

This librarian sits us at a table and actually brings us books himself.

We read. And look at hideous photos. One book says some vitiligo victims feel like freaks and withdraw from social situations. I close it. It's the biology I want to read, not some depressing psychology junk.

I open another book. Dr. Ratner was right. No one knows what brings on vitiligo. No one knows how to cure it. But they try. They try really hard.

There's the blunt and painful method: skin grafting. But you keep getting new spots. And the grafted skin can get spots.

There's an ultraviolet light therapy to darken the spots. You put a photosensitive medication on the spots first, then sit under a lamp that shoots UV light. Two to four times a week, for fifteen to thirty minutes, for a year or more. And then sometimes it doesn't work at all.

After each treatment you have to wear UV protection over your eyes for a few days or you might get cataracts. So you're wearing the protection nearly all the time. And you have to wash the drug off your skin before you go outside or else cover up really good, because you can get a terrible sunburn.

I am not interested in UV therapy. Laser therapy sounds even worse—the burns are apparently super painful, they can't be exposed to the sun, and sometimes it works and sometimes it doesn't.

But I have to find a cure. Okay, here's more.

If a person has severe vitiligo, where over fifty percent of the body is white patches, then doctors can use a skin bleach, so the person becomes whiter all over. Then you look more uniform. The trouble is, the bleaching is permanent. But sometimes vitiligo clears up on its own, so you've become a ghost for no reason.

Sometimes vitiligo clears up on its own. I'm trembling inside.

Mamma obsesses on bad things pretty often and Dad always tells her that statistically it just isn't going to happen to us. And Mamma always answers that if it happens even to a tiny fraction of people, why shouldn't we be in that tiny fraction. But it can't just be the doomed tiny fraction that our family should be part of. We could be part of the lucky tiny fraction, too. Why not?

I keep reading.

Ointments can be used—Vitamin D, cortisone, tacrolimus. They don't have a lot of side effects. And sometimes they help. But mostly they don't.

The one thing that has no side effect is cosmetic concealers. Covermark, Dermablend, Chromelin Complexion Blender. It turns out most people with vitiligo cover it up; they go into hiding. All these white-speckled people, hiding away like fugitives. That strikes me as ridiculous. I'd never do that. I am who I am.

Except lipstick is a cover-up.

I'm getting dizzy.

And, hey, it turns out I need vitamins now. I should take a B complex, and E, and folic acid, and ascorbic acid, every day.

And I shouldn't develop film. Exposure to phenols can accelerate vitiligo. Well, there goes that future hobby—as though anyone develops film anymore. I bet I can't become a horse jockey, either. Or a dentist. Or the president of a small banana republic.

"I want to go home."

"Sure." Mamma closes the book she's reading.

We drive home with the radio on. I stare at the back of my hand. Is there a white spot there? I cover it with the tip of my index finger, then lift and look again. It's still there. It wasn't there this morning. It wasn't there at lunch.

Vitiligo happens gradually for most people. But for others it comes in a bang. White lips one morning. Unrecognizable three months later.

When we pull into the driveway, I turn the radio off. "I'm not doing anything with UV therapy or lasers. And no skin grafts. And no bleach."

"Let's see what Dr. Ratner says."

"I'm not doing it, Mamma."

"It's your decision, Pina. Anyway, maybe it will just clear up on its own." Her chin is lifted high. In profile like this, she looks more than pretty. Her cheeks are a little bit apple-y, but that keeps her looking young. Her nose is small, her lips are full. I bet she always expected to have a good-looking daughter. Not a patchy, blotchy one.

I check the back of my hand. That's a white spot for sure. I put the tip of my index finger on it—it doesn't cover it anymore.

I don't have the heart to show Mamma.

14

I CLOSE THE DOOR behind Mr. and Mrs. Harrison and turn around to face Sarah. "So, are you still in trouble?"

"That was yesterday."

I smile. "What do you want to do?"

"Legos."

That makes me smile even wider. Mrs. Harrison is not a stupid woman or a bad mother. But somehow she got the idea that building blocks were boys' toys. So I gave Sarah Legos for her third birthday. Now it's her favorite thing. And the Harrisons have done their good-parent thing and filled a gigantic basket with them. There must be nine hundred in this basket. Maybe more. Of course more. Extravagance is the name of the good-parent game.

We dump out a bunch and build, side by side on the floor. I like this.

"So, how's nursery school?"

"Bill can roll under the radiator."

"There isn't enough room under radiators."

"There is for Bill."

"Even if Bill has a body like Flat Stanley's, his head would never fit."

Sarah looks up at me, a Lego in each hand. "I mash his head."

"Oh." I chew at a hangnail. "Is Bill a person?"

"No, dummy. A person can't roll under the radiator." She laughs.

I wonder if Bill is lurking under the radiator here, or if he's still at nursery school. And what is he anyway? But I might as well go with the flow. I add a Lego in a precarious spot.

"Want to watch *Jeopardy*?"

I blink in surprise. "Is it on now?"

"It's always on. Daddy loves to watch."

"Do you like it?"

"No."

"Why do you want to watch it?"

"I thought you would want to."

"That's very thoughtful of you, Sarah."

"Then I can do what I want."

"I thought you wanted to build with Legos."

"Want to cook?"

Did my stomach growl? I will raid the refrigerator after Sarah gets in bed. "No, thank you."

"I'll turn on *Jeopardy* for you."

I put my cell on the coffee table and set it to flash green if there's a message, so it won't be as likely to disturb Sarah. This is wishful thinking. No one will text me. Everyone I know is at Becca's party. Except maybe Owen.

But there is the slight chance that Devin might decide to text me before she leaves the house. I didn't get to apologize to her today. I was going to, after school—but then Mamma showed up and we spent all that time at the medical library. I didn't even get to have dinner before I had to come over here to babysit.

Sarah touches the cell. "Are you going to send messages?"

I nod. "You're right. I'm the one who should send a message."

"To Devin?"

"Yes."

"She's still your best friend?"

"Yes."

"Rucka is my best friend."

"That's an unusual name."

"I made it up."

"Oh. Does she like it when you call her Rucka?"

"She runs away."

"Maybe you shouldn't call her Rucka."

"Can I send a message?"

"It's hard."

"Daddy lets me type on his computer."

"It's harder with a cell phone, Sarah."

She screws up her mouth and I think she's going to throw a fit. Instead, she says, "I'll do Legos. You do *Jeopardy*."

"Can't I do Legos with you?"

"I guess."

So we're back on the floor building with Legos. We work in silence. It's a relief. We build houses and vehicles and a wall all around. It's turning into a little town.

I look at my watch. "Yikes, it's late. Want a bath?"

Sarah gets up and runs to the bathroom, stripping as she goes.

I pick up the clothes and throw them in the hamper and run her a tub.

She dumps the net bag of sea creatures into the water and I tell her about the frenetic life of tunas. I don't know if she's listening. She's half-singing to herself.

She finishes and I dry her off. She puts on her pj's and races off while I drain the tub. Then she chooses three books and we sit on her bed and I read all three.

I kiss her good night.

"Let's go see if you have a message."

I look at my watch. "It's late. And, anyway, everyone I know is at a party. No one's going to send me a message."

"Let's make a bet."

"What kind of bet?"

"If you got a message, I get to stay up till midnight."

"Midnight? Sarah, have you ever been up till midnight?"

"I took a nap today. So I can stay up."

"I didn't get a message. I'm sure of it."

"Yes you did."

"How do you know?"

"I saw."

"What did you see?"

"Your cell lit up."

Oh. So that's where she went when I was emptying the tub. I should explain to her that making a bet when you know the answer already is cheating. But first I want to see who sent a message. I go out to the living room with Sarah at my heels.

It's Joshua Winer. "where r u?"

The jitters come so hard, I practically drop the phone.

"I told you." Sarah points. "Is it Devin?"

"No."

"Can I answer for you?"

"No."

"Can I play more?"

"Yes. At Legos. Where I can see you."

Sarah sits back down with the Legos.

I type: "babysitting. where r u?"

"ur there!   finally. address?"

Address?

I type: "Y?"

"dont u want me 2 stop by?"

I hug myself. I don't even know him. Well, what a stupid thought. Of course I know him. But the him I know is six years younger. All I know of this him is that we talked two days at lunch. We texted once. That's the sum total. And that's nothing.

I stare at the words. They're bold. All at once I'm mad. "do u want 2?"

"y not?"

There are tons of reasons why not. I type: "Im busy."

"r u mad at me?"

Yeah. Yeah, I'm mad at Joshua Winer. And at Dr. Ratner. And at my parents. And at the whole world. I'm about to turn off the cell, when another message comes.

"I didnt mean to act dumb. Sorry. Im no good at this. Look, I want to come. But if you dont, thats cool."

There's something dear about the way he wrote that. Direct and open. No bullshit. And he used ordinary typing, like in a real letter or something just without the apostrophes—he hasn't done that in his other texting. He's still Joshua, and I like Joshua. I like him a lot. I type fast before I have time to think better of it: "244 Lincoln. 2 houses down from mine." I send it, then wonder for a second if he remembers where my house is. There's no way I would forget where his is.

"See you soon."

He remembers.

Of course he remembers. He texted me—that means he kept my phone number all these years. What an idiot I am.

I hug myself again. And I rock back and forth on the couch. I check my watch.

I sit on the floor and build with Sarah. I don't even know what I'm building. Maybe it's a never-ending wall. Lego after Lego snaps into place and moves off toward infinity. We build forever.

The doorbell rings.

"Hey." Joshua Winer stands there with his hands in his jacket pockets. It's not cool enough for a jacket, even a light one like that. And I realize he's always got a jacket on.

He started that in middle school—when he got popular. Maybe that's his Mr. Cool badge. "It's been a while," he says.

"Twelve minutes."

He blinks. "Is that how long I'm allowed?"

"That's how long it took you to get here."

"You're not Devin," says Sarah, coming up beside me.

"I'm Joshua. Who are you?"

"Sarah. This is my house."

"Then I'll do what you say."

"Watch *Jeopardy* with Sep."

"All right, Boss."

"I'm Sarah."

"All right, Sarah."

Sarah points and we sit on the couch obediently.

I watch TV but I don't see anything. Maybe I'm going blind instead of deaf. This is a very bad idea. I should have never given him the address. "Why . . . ?" I can't finish.

"Why what?"

I have to blink back tears. "Just why."

"I take it this isn't a huge philosophical question."

I shake my head.

"So . . . you're asking about . . . right now?"

"You're here. Why?"

Joshua nods his head slowly. "I wanted to see you."

"Why?"

I see his Adam's apple move as he swallows. "I don't know." He looks sideways at me. Then he turns to look at me head-on, shifting so one leg rests, knee cocked, between us. "I wanted to . . . I don't know . . . I wanted to get to know you. Like we used to."

"Why?" I manage to say it without my voice cracking.

He blinks. "You haven't changed that much, I guess. You never made anything easy."

"Nothing is easy."

He scratches his temple with just one finger. He looks so puzzled, I actually feel sorry for him. But I need to know. I don't want to be miserable, and I'm pretty sure that Joshua Winer could make me miserable if I let myself fall for him. He wouldn't mean to—I can bet that—but it would happen anyway.

He drops his hand. It falls in his lap on top of his other hand with a little smack. I flinch at this proof of the weight of him, the physicality. A sharp smell hangs on him. Aftershave? It kind of zings me. I sit taller. His nose is straight and long. His eyebrows are dark brown, like his hair. It's not as dark as mine, but it's close.

I realize he's looking at me looking at him. But he's not challenging me. His eyes are just nice. Easy. I like their light, flickering color. I swallow again and I'm pretty sure I'm not going to cry now. That's passed, at least.

"Blue lipstick," he says at last. "Are you going to experiment with every color?"

"I'm trying to hide white."

"There's nothing wrong with white."

"How do you know?"

"Sep, I have no idea what we're talking about."

All over again I'm on the verge of tears. This is so stupid. He's here. I might as well try to have a nice time. "What would you like to talk about?" I ask.

"Something I know."

"Something you know?"

"Yeah. That way I can be sure to have something to say."

"How's football?"

"Good. That I can talk about. Sure."

"Want to take your jacket off first? You know, stay a while?"

He throws his jacket over the back of the couch. And he talks. About practice every day. About the game tomorrow night. About the lineup and where he fits and what he wants to achieve this fall. He's totally into it and his hands move as he talks. Big, wide hands. There's a scar on his right palm. I don't remember that scar.

Now he's smiling at me.

"What?" I say.

"You haven't said a word. That's not like the Sep I knew."

"I've been listening. I didn't know you were so . . . loquacious. You didn't use to be. Or am I remembering wrong?"

"Tell me about you."

I open my mouth and dance comes out. I hadn't planned that, but somehow it just fits with all Joshua's talk about football. I tell about Ms. Martin and Jazz Dance Club and how sometimes when she talks about wings I feel like I have them. And then I stop. I don't want to be talking anymore. "That's all. That's all I have to say."

"Nice." Joshua bobs his head in agreement. "Hey, where's the kid? Sarah?"

Oh my God, I forgot about Sarah. "Sarah?"

"Quiet," calls Sarah from the kitchen.

I go in with Joshua at my side.

Sarah's sitting on the floor. There's an open egg carton on the stool. And a broken egg on the floor beside her. "Shhhh!" she says.

"What are you doing?" I whisper.

"Sitting."

"Why is there a broken egg on the floor?"

"It had a bad shell."

"Did you smash it?"

"I sat on it."

"Why?"

"So it would hatch."

I'm getting it. "Are you sitting on an egg now?"

"Yes."

"Is it broken?"

"I don't know. My bottoms are wet from the last egg."

"Hens sit on eggs, not people. People crush eggs."

"Not good eggs. Good eggs are strong."

"Get up, Sarah. Please."

Sarah stands up. The egg is whole. Is it made of marble?

"That's a good egg," says Sarah.

"That's an amazing egg," says Joshua.

"All right. I'll put an X on it. With this pencil. And tomorrow, when your mother is home, you can ask her if you can sit on it more. But for now, it's going in the refrigerator and you're going back in the tub."

She doesn't fight me. This is weird. Sarah typically fights on principle. I get her washed up and into fresh pj's and back in bed with Howl Doo under her arm.

"I want to say good night to Joshua."

"All right." I go to the door and call Joshua.

He comes padding down the hall quickly, eyes wide, like an obedient but bewildered dog wondering what he'll have to do to please the master.

"Sarah wants to say good night to you."

Joshua goes to stand at the side of Sarah's bed. "Good night, Sport."

"I'm Sarah."

"Good night, Sarah."

"You're big."

"I play football."

"Daddy watches football on TV."

"You have a smart daddy. And a nice dog there."

"He's a wolf." She holds up Howl Doo. "His name is Howl Doo."

"He's terrific."

"If you like him so much, you can join his fan club on Facebook."

"I'll think about it."

"Good night, Joshua," says Sarah.

I leave with Joshua at my heels, and head for the kitchen to clean the floor, but Joshua's already taken care of that. "Thanks."

He shrugs, but I can see he's proud of himself. "She's fun."

"I'll give her mother your number."

He laughs. "Not that much fun."

"I'm hungry. Want to watch me raid the refrigerator?"

"Won't Sarah's parents get mad?"

"You've never babysat before, have you?"

"How could you tell?"

"It's the job of the babysitter to scarf down anything good. You hungry?"

"Always." He opens a cupboard.

"Look for nuts."

"You like nuts?"

"They have copper. Only it might make me schizo. Oh, look, here's some good ham."

"I'm Jewish, remember?"

And of course I remember. But I don't ever remember him refusing food before. If anything, he was a pig when he was little. "So you don't eat pork?"

He grins. "Sure I eat it. But if you're allowed to say schizo when there's no real connection, I'm allowed to say Jewish."

"But you are Jewish. So does that mean you think I'm schizo?"

He looks at my face for a moment. Almost appraisingly. "You really are different from how you used to be."

"You mean when we were in fifth grade?"

"Well, that, sure. But last year, too."

Last year? He noticed me last year? "Really?"

"I don't know. You look different."

I'm not about to touch that one. "Want pickle slices in your sandwich?"

"Does the Pope have a big nose?"

"I think it's supposed to be 'Is the Pope Catholic?'—but it doesn't matter anyway, because I don't know anything about the Pope. I'm not Catholic."

"Your mom's Italian and you're not Catholic?"

"Mamma's not really Italian."

"Oh, come on. Don't treat me like I'm a stranger. She was born in Italy. You showed me on a map exactly where."

"She left more than twenty years ago. If you look at the way she dresses, you know she's not Italian. Italian women have style." I finish making the sandwich and push the plate along the counter toward him. "Eat."

He takes a bite. "Spicy mustard. Good."

"Where were you at lunch on Thursday?" There. I asked it.

"The team ate together. We had a few things to figure out before practice." He takes another bite and talks with his mouth full: "Where were you at lunch today?"

He looked for me today? I gag on a bite. "I had to go to the library. I skipped lunch."

"That's why you're so hungry."

"And dinner."

"You skipped dinner, too?" He sounds appalled. "Want me to make you a second sandwich?"

"This is enough."

"I saw a box of cookies in the cupboard," he says.

"I hate junk food. I always have." I jut my chin out at him. "You're the one who used to munch chips all the time."

"Not anymore. It ruins my game. No junk food. No alcohol. No drugs."

"You're like an ad."

"I'm trying to be."

My cheeks burn. He's so earnest. And I realize he was like that in fifth grade, too. Everyone was sort of earnest in those days—but he was extreme. We had that in common. We understood each other somehow.

We finish and wash everything and put it away. All the evidence gone.

"I'll be back." I go to the bathroom and check my lipstick. It's still okay. I take toilet paper and blot it—something I read about online. Nothing comes off. Maybe this lipstick has become a permanent stain.

When I come out, Joshua is sitting on the couch again. He's big and quiet. He has thin cheeks. Thin cheeks look good on him. Thin cheeks look fantastic on him.

I walk over and stand there looking down at him and feeling like a stupid blob.

He pats the cushion beside him.

I refuse to think. I refuse to hope. I sit down.

His lip twitches like he almost smiled. But nicely. Everything he does is so nice. He pats closer to him.

I move closer. I'm breathing hard.

His face comes close to mine. The scent of spicy mustard is strong. But we share it—we smell the same. Spicy mustard can be "our" scent—like some couples have a song. What would he say if I suggested it?

We're not a couple.

I look down at the back of my hand. At the white spot that I've checked at least nine hundred times since I first saw it. It's bigger than a nickel now. White lips and one spot on a hand. Not so bad. But it could be so much more, so soon. It could be horrific.

"Will you look at me?"

I look at him, feeling stupid.

His face comes closer. But slowly. Very, very slowly. As though he isn't really moving.

"Are you okay?" His breath stirs the little hairs above my lip.

He's like a curve on a graph. Like in geometry. And I'm like an asymptote. A line he approaches. I'm his limit. Has he stopped? I can feel his body heat. And all I know is that I want. I want so much. This is unbearable. I may die. I know this is a mess. I know this is bad timing. Vitiligo

vitiligo vitiligo. But can't I have just a little something good first? Just a kiss? One kiss? "You get closer and closer," I whisper, "but you never get there."

"I'll get there if you want me to."

This is really happening. If I want it to. If I don't go flying away toward infinity. If I don't tell him the truth. But I have to tell him. I have to. "Your eyes are gray-green."

"Yours are rich chocolate."

"Your skin is tan from all that football practice."

He smiles. "Your skin is like a giant olive. I love olives."

I swallow. "I'm changing color."

He blinks. "I think I got that. With the lipstick stuff."

"It's more than that."

"Okay."

"Okay? Is that all you have to say?"

"I . . . I don't know. We've been talking a lot. I was sort of hoping we could try not talking. For a little while. Do you think we could try that? Try not talking?"

"There's something I should probably tell you."

"For a little while? Not talking just a little while? Could we try it?"

His lips are so close to mine I can almost feel them. Like a force. Only he isn't forcing anything. He asks so nicely I could cry.

He puts a hand on my cheek.

I want to press against his hand. I want to move my lips to his. I want, I want. He's so close I can hardly see him. Like a blur.

His lips move to my other cheek. They brush softly back and forth and now from the center of my cheek toward my mouth. And they press on mine just the slightest.

And I'm kissing him, too, soft, miraculously soft. Oh, thank you, thank everything that is good and bright.

But now my hands are on the sides of his head, moving on their own, and I'm kissing his forehead and temples and cheeks and eyelids and nose. I'm out of control, kissing so fast. I think I'm going to pass out, but I don't—and I can't stop. I must be crazy. And we're kissing on the lips again and it's not soft anymore. And all that matters is knowing his lips.

He stands up and pulls me with him and I've never been handled like this before, or not since I was a little girl, and it feels good to be moved around, to have someone in charge, and his eyes stay on mine and I know he's asking, but silently, asking, and he lies down, taking me with him, and I'm on top, our full lengths hugging. My breath is short and there is nothing, nothing anywhere ever, as good as these kisses.

15

I TYPE: "NEED 2 TALK."

Devin answers: "y?"

She's been like this. It took nine hundred texts all morning to even get her to answer. I type: "need to talk."

There's a long wait.

Finally, Devin answers: "k."

Good. "ur house in 5." I race down the stairs.

"What's the rush, Slut?" Dante's leaning into the closet under the stairs where he keeps his skateboard.

I zip over and kiss him on the cheek. He goes to rub it off, but I catch his wrist. "If you rub, you'll just smear Hazelnut lipstick all over."

"Great. So now I have to go wash my face."

"Keep it. Maybe the guys will think you have a secret lover. You can pretend you're the coolest ninth grader ever."

"What's going on? You've been grumpy all week. Now you're acting happy."

"Wow. I guess you're right. Kill me."

He shrugs. "You can be happy if you want."

I leave.

I can be happy if I want.

Last night Joshua said he'd get there if I wanted him to.

What I want and what I can have—there's such a gulf in there, no matter what Dante and Joshua say. But right now, this moment, I'm concentrating on what I want.

Devin's walking toward me on the sidewalk. Good old Devin. Best friend Devin. I run and hug her and my heart's beating so hard, I can't hear anything. I'm spinning with her around and around.

She laughs. "Whoa! What's going on, Sep?"

That's just what Dante asked me.

"I have something to tell you."

"I'm listening."

"I know I've been a jerk all week. I'm sorry."

Devin's eyes cloud. "You were snobby. Like you thought you were better than me."

"What? I would never think that. I was PMS-ing and then there's been, well, stuff going on."

"It's okay."

"Really?"

"Yeah." She smiles. "Hey, want to hear about Becca's party?"

"Sure."

"It wasn't horrible. I swear. Everyone was there. Not the whole time, but people kept coming in and out all night. And I danced with lots of people." She pauses. "And with Charlie." That last part comes out like a cross between an announcement and an admission.

"Really?"

"Yeah. He wasn't boring."

"I never thought he was. You're the one who always said that."

"He was nice."

"Nice? Like nice nice?"

She nods, her head bobbing like a toy Buddha on a dashboard.

"Good." I grin. "That's good, Devin. He's had his eye on you for a long time."

She shrugs again. "You think so?"

"I know so."

"Well . . . where were you, anyway?"

"I babysat Sarah."

"Babysat? What's the matter with you? You didn't go to the party just to take care of that little monster?"

"She's not that bad. She's just a handful. And I had a good time."

"A good time with Sarah?"

"Someone came over."

"Someone came over?"

"Joshua."

"Joshua? Joshua Winer? You don't mean Joshua Winer?"

"He's nice."

She looks stupefied. "Nice?"

I laugh. "Juicy."

"I don't believe this."

"Why not? We used to be friends."

"God, do I know. I was jealous of him all fifth grade. You played with him more than you played with me. I think I actually hated him. But then he turned into a giant snob in sixth grade. And I was so glad."

"He's not a giant snob now."

"Clearly. So what happened?"

"We talked."

"And?"

"We kissed."

"You made out with Joshua Winer? Joshua Winer,

Joshua Winer? One of the most popular guys in school? Captain of the football team?"

Joshua is captain of the team. He got chosen at the end of last year. I forgot that. I actually forgot that, I'm so stupid about those things. Captain, and he's only a junior. "I guess so. Yeah."

"Oh my God."

"Yeah. Oh my God. And my lipstick didn't even come off."

"You made out with Joshua Winer and you worried about your lipstick? What are you, crazy?"

"Maybe."

"When did this happen?"

"Last night."

"No, I mean when did the two of you start liking each other?"

"I don't know. He just kind of appeared. In the lunch-room a couple of days. Then at Sarah's house."

"And you didn't tell me anything?"

"I'm telling you now. There was nothing to tell before now."

"What about Sharon Parker?"

"I don't know." It's my turn to shrug.

"You didn't ask him?"

"No."

Devin tilts her head. "Well, that might be dumb. You want to know, right?"

"Did you see her last night?"

"Her crowd didn't come."

"Joshua did. But he left."

"To see you." Devin's mouth twists in worry. "So when are you going to see him again?"

"That's the thing, Devin. There's a game tonight. Want to go with me?"

"So you can jilt me when it's over?"

I laugh. "Something like that. He asked if he could see me afterwards."

"I can't believe it. This feels like the old days—you and Joshua, and me on the outside looking in."

"Oh! Oh, I didn't mean it that way." What an idiot I was to laugh. "You're right, of course. I don't want to be one of those stupid girls who gets a boyfriend and then forgets everyone else. But . . ."

"Shut up. I was joking. If he wants to see you afterwards, you'll go with him. And that's how it should be."

"Thanks. And it won't be lots of times, I promise. He's not going to be with me long. It might just be tonight and that's it."

"Don't say that. You'll doom it at the start."

"It's already doomed." I hold the back of my hand in front of her eyes. I should say something, but I can't talk. My stupid tongue has gone flabby. My eyes sting. And there's that heartburn again.

"What's that? That white spot?"

I swallow.

Then I tell her.

16

"WELL IF IT ISN'T Slut and Friend of Slut." Dante walks into the backyard and looks down at us. We're lying on the old picnic blanket. Dante was smiling at first, but now that he's seen us, his face changes. The smile is still there, as if pasted on—it's his eyes that give him away. They look a bit frantic. Sort of like a startled wild animal. He clearly thinks he's caught us doing something totally whack. He glances over at the bottle beside us. "Is that my Selsun Blue?"

Rattle wakes from whatever grog-land he was in, stands, and bumps into Dante's legs in greeting.

"You can have it back. We didn't take much."

Dante points at me. He wags his finger as though he's going to talk. Then he picks up the bottle and walks toward the house. Then he turns around and walks back. "Why did you two put dandruff shampoo on your lips?"

"Not just lips. I put it on the spot on my hand, too. There's a chance I have a fungus under my skin instead of vitiligo. From what I read, it's probably close to a point zero zero one chance. But I'm humoring Dr. Ratner, because these days I need people to humor me and I figure what goes around comes around or whatever that saying is. Your shampoo could kill the fungus."

He looks slightly relieved. "Why aren't you doing this in the privacy of the bathroom?"

"The sun has its part."

"About the bathroom . . . ," Dante scratches the back of his neck. "Do you have to leave your stool sample thingamajig on the back of the toilet?"

"I only have one day left. But I'll move it."

"Thanks. Tim and Zach are coming over. They like you for some odd reason, but they don't like you that much." Dante keeps standing there, looking at us. His forehead wrinkles. "Hey, Friend of Slut, do you have white lips, too? I thought this thing wasn't contagious."

Devin smiles wickedly. "Want to kiss me and find out, big boy?"

Dante jumps backward, but he might be only half kidding.

I laugh. "Don't freak, Squirt. It's not contagious. You won't get it. Devin's just being my friend, doing what I have to do."

"I wouldn't put shampoo on my lips for a friend."

"It's called solidarity. It's a girl thing."

"I wouldn't ask a friend to put shampoo on his lips for me."

"I didn't ask. That's the whole point of solidarity. You don't have to ask."

"Yeah, that sounds like a girl thing, all right. All those unspoken messages."

"Well, well, well," says Devin. "Is that the voice of experience? Has little Dante been talking with girls? Do you have a girlfriend?"

Dante strikes a beefcake pose. "All the girls are my friends."

"Oooo." Devin claps her hands.

He laughs. "Sep, you better get your solidarity ass up to the kitchen, 'cause Mom wants you peeling peaches."

Peach chores. I love our peaches. But the first week of September is always a giant pain because all the peaches come ripe within days of each other.

"I'll help." Devin stands up and brushes off the back of

her pants. "It's been almost a half hour anyway. And you said it wasn't a good idea to go over."

"You don't want to help, believe me. 'Peeling peaches' doesn't mean just peeling peaches. It means washing them, cutting out the rot, peeling, pitting, cutting into small pieces, and freezing in containers that hold just the right amount for pies."

"I love your mom's peach pies."

"All nine hundred of them? Come on, let's go wash our lips."

Five minutes later we're in the kitchen. My cell is heavy in my pocket. Devin already texted Charlie. He answered her immediately. I get the distinct feeling that Devin is on her way to getting what she's been waiting for her whole life. It seems so obvious. And so simple.

Envy makes my stomach churn. That's what I want: simple.

We peel and pit. Devin really is into solidarity.

Dante and Tim and Zach zip through the kitchen at random intervals, stealing peaches. It pisses me off when they steal the ones we've already prepared for freezing. But it doesn't really matter.

The cell in my pocket is silent.

We cut and put peaches in containers and pop them into the freezer.

Charlie and Devin texted each other already this morning. But Charlie and Devin aren't Joshua and me. Every couple is different.

Joshua and me—oh my God—we aren't even a couple. I don't know what we are. I don't know what last night was. Kisses are no big deal to some people.

We're deep into the bucket of peaches when my cell finally beeps. Devin shrieks. "It's him. He texted you."

I take out my cell. She's right. I read: "hey, lips."

Lips. This is awful. I type: "dont call me that."

"what should i call u?"

I type: "Sep."

"r u mad at me?"

I type: "no."

"really?"

I type: "really."

"see u tonite?"

I type: "yes."

"i miss u."

I hesitate.

"Go on," says Devin. She's leaning over my shoulder. "Say you miss him, too."

"You shouldn't even be reading this."

"Come on, I'd let you."

"I didn't read what you and Charlie wrote."

"You could have if you wanted to. I didn't stop you."

"Please, Devin?"

She looks at me with her mouth all pressed shut tight. "I need to get home anyway. I better do my Spanish now if I'm going to be a good friend and go with you to the football game."

"You're trying to guilt me out."

"Oh, you mean just because you're going to jilt me there?" She smiles, washes her hands, and leaves.

Another message from Joshua: "u ok?"

I type: "i miss u too."

"thats what i wanted to hear. what color r ur lips today?"

I'm so glad I put lipstick back on. I type: "brown."

"chocolate?"

I type: "hazelnut."

There's a long pause.

Then: "didnt u say nuts make u schizo?"

I type: "i dont eat my lipstick."

"i might."

My stomach flips. I type: "its just a color—not a flavor."

"ur own flavor is best anyway."

My upper arms are all pin prickles. I have to press my knees together to keep them from shaking. This is absurd. I type: "stop there."

"k. later."

I go back to processing peaches.

What am I doing, getting romantic with a guy who's going to be repulsed by me in a couple of months? Or sooner. I should tell him. Now. Or, if I don't have the courage to tell him, I should walk away from him. Now. Only I don't want to. I really, really don't want to. I want this to last.

And I know it can't.

After peaches, I translate Ovid. The passage is about the nymph Daphne. The god Apollo decides he wants to have her and he chases her, the big, galumphing rapist. As she flees, she calls to her father for help. So the father turns her into a laurel tree. And Ovid has the nerve to praise the transformation because it preserves her loveliness.

Poor Daphne, forever a tree.

What kind of father can't think of anything better to do than that? If he's so good with trees, he could have made a forest sprout up, hiding her.

Or he could have had trees sprout up and surround Apollo so he was locked away.

Or he could have made Daphne ugly so Apollo would forget about her. He could have stricken her with vitiligo.

Maybe I should drop Latin III, too. Only it's too late now. Friday was the last day to change classes.

I finish reading *Their Eyes Were Watching God* and I feel better. Zora Neale Hurston is better than Ovid.

I get up and pace. I straighten my desk, put away pencils and pens, line up books. I pick a shirt off the back of my chair and carry it to the laundry hamper. I fiddle with the broken pull on my blinds. I need to stay busy, to not think about Joshua. Be a swift. Be a tuna.

Only nothing can keep me from thinking about how I'm lying to Joshua.

No, I'm not. There's a difference between lying and not telling everything.

I touch my lips and they come alive. We kissed. We kissed and kissed and kissed.

My eyes burn.

There's no good way out.

17

I LEAN TOWARD DEVIN'S ear. "They're fighting down there. Look! Ouch!"

Devin glances around nervously. We are squashed in the bleachers near the hot dog stand, surrounded by football fans. "Whisper!"

"I am whispering."

"Whisper quieter. You sound like a moron."

The crowd cheers. The guys on the field are in a big pile again.

Devin pushes back the cuticles on her left hand and keeps looking around. I don't get why she's so on edge. No one can hear us with all this yelling.

"I don't like football." And I feel disloyal, because this is what matters to Joshua.

"Come on, Sep," she hisses in my ear. "We've gone to games before and you've always liked them."

"Maybe I never watched closely before. Look at them. They're smashing into each other. They could get hurt for real."

"It's part of the sport."

"Where's the sportsmanship in that?"

The crowd boos and groans. I look out at the field. I can't see the numbers on their uniforms; I can't see 22. Well, that's okay. If I could, I'd wince every time Joshua got jumped on. This way, I don't even know. And now I realize why I'm being so critical—I don't want Joshua hurt. I don't want those big guys jumping on him. Joshua's tall, but not as hefty as some of them.

"Dumb official!" screams the guy next to me. He looks older than my father. "Bad call, bad call!" I bet it was his son the call was made on.

"Look at that guy. He's all mad. Maybe everyone is. Maybe no one's having fun."

Devin wrinkles her nose. "Everyone's having fun but you. Look around. See who's with who. Let's talk about that." She cranes her neck. "See Raquel? I bet that T-shirt is a child's size six, it's so tight. Oh!" Devin looks toward the hot dog stand.

"Are you hungry?"

Then I see him: Charlie. Tall and willowy—as unlike a football player as anyone could be. No one's going to tackle him—he's safe.

I glance out at the field. Guys are getting into some lineup. Maybe they're going to bash each other again. I wish Joshua would sit it out a while. And good grief, he would be horrified if he heard my thoughts; he loves this game.

I look back at Charlie. He's scanning the bleachers. When he spies Devin, he smiles and waves.

She waves back and practically bounces on her seat.

"Did you tell him you were coming?" I ask.

"Yeah."

"Did you plan to meet up with him?"

"Sort of."

"So is this a reverse—are you the one jilting me?"

"Yeah. Unless you mind." And I know she means it— she'd never ditch me if I asked her not to. She's standing now. Waving again.

A chill comes. But this is her chance. "Go for it."

"Really?"

"Of course."

"I'm already gone. Good luck." She puts her mouth to my ear. "Don't get pregnant."

"Funny. Very, very funny."

Devin picks her way through feet and knees to the end of the row, and she and Charlie go up to a high row where there's still space for couples.

I'm exposed. Alone. Just me and my thoughts.

Well, there are ways to kill thoughts.

I step over the hurdles to the end of the row, just like Devin did. People grumble, asking why I didn't go past them when my friend went so I wouldn't disturb them twice. I mumble apologies.

I buy a hot dog and smear on the smallest bit of yellow mustard. Food trumps thought any day.

Someone bumps into me and my barely eaten hot dog goes flying to the ground.

"Oops." Crystal Lewis points at my hot dog and giggles.

Sharon Parker stumbles beside her. She doesn't even look at the hot dog, but she giggles anyway and says, "Oopsh."

I smell alcohol on them. I think it's wine, but really the only drink I can recognize for sure is beer. This isn't beer.

They walk a bit wobbly toward the Porta-Potties. You'd have to be major drunk to walk like that. Or maybe they're putting on a show.

It was Crystal who bumped into me. So why do I feel like it happened on purpose? Could Sharon know Joshua was with me last night?

Sharon's long brown hair, much lighter than mine, is wavy rather than curly. Her face is classically pretty—small nose, fine lips, thin cheeks. I touch my own face with my fingertips. We're nothing alike.

I buy another hot dog, and this time I put on sauerkraut and beans and top it all with heaps of mustard. It's good.

The far end of the bleachers is fairly empty, so that's where I head. I sit high up and eat slowly. When I finish, I watch the game. Thankfully there are lot of time-outs, when nothing happens.

The laces on my right sneaker hang loose. I carefully take one end and pull it out of all the holes except the very last one. Then I tie a figure-eight knot in it. Then an over-hand knot. And a double overhand. A slipknot. Then a running knot. Now a taut line hitch. When I was in Girl Scouts we didn't do knots. But Dante's Boy Scout troop did, and he taught me.

I undo all the knots and re-lace my shoe and tie it and try to watch the game.

It's dark now. The spot on the back of my hand doesn't show.

The game finally ends. We won. There's a lot of jumping

and cheering and hugging and people clapping each other on the back. And that's just in the stands. Out on the field the players are being mauled by fans.

The crowd leaves, but there are lingerers.

Gradually even they leave. The lights at the entrance to the stands go out.

And Joshua Winer walks this way. There's no one else around, so he's definitely coming toward me. His helmet's in one hand. The pads on his shoulders and legs make him look like he shouldn't be able to move so gracefully, but here he comes, kind of loping, like an animal that feels at home in the night. I brush the hair back from my face. My breath is already a quiet pant. He comes around the side of the bleachers and reaches up and puts his free hand on my shoe. "Hey."

"Hey, yourself, Joshua Winer."

"Last names, huh? We getting formal?" His hand cups the top of my shoe and squeezes a little.

"Good game?" I ask.

"Didn't you watch it?"

"Sort of. I mean, I was here."

He laughs. "Yeah. It was okay. In fact, it was really good. So what did you do, if you didn't watch the game?"

"I tied knots. In my shoelace. A half hour, maybe more, counted out in loops and twists."

He puts his helmet on the ground, then holds out his palm to me. "Got a pen?"

"Sure." I dig in my purse and hand him my favorite rollerball pen.

Joshua unties the bow on my right shoe. Then he unlaces it. It's just a shoe, that's all, it doesn't even cover anything personal. But as he pulls the lace free of each hole, a shock wave goes up my body. I feel like he's undressing me. I cross my arms over my chest and bury my hands in my armpits. And I'm aware suddenly that he's covered in sweat. He gives off the smell of hard work. It's a good thing my hands are pinned down, 'cause I have the urge to put them in his hair.

He leaves the lace still in the last hole, just like I did, and he attaches my pen with a neat chain hitch. He tilts his head at me. "Knots are meant to do work."

"Smarty-pants." I open my purse and take out my lip color. I attach it with a timber hitch.

"Nice. Got a key?"

I hand him my front door key, which dangles from a Rutgers University key chain—my dad's alma mater.

He attaches the key with a clove hitch.

I feel inside my purse and come up with a pencil. I attach it with two half hitches. "That's it. We're out of lace."

"That doesn't mean you won."

"I like ties," I say.

"Spoken like someone who doesn't do sports."

"Knots aren't sports."

"Right." He undoes all the knots, hands me my belongings, and re-laces my shoe. I feel like a little kid—and I remember how he practically lifted me last night, how he moved me so I was lying on top of him. I was wrong; I don't feel like a little kid at all. My insides tighten.

He finishes lacing and ties a bow. Then he folds both hands behind my right ankle and rests his chin on top of my shoe and looks up at me. "Knots are good, Sep. But sports can be, too." He gives a coaxing smile. "If you watch them."

I laugh now, but his hands are on my ankle and they're warm and it's hard to think beyond that. "I'll try harder next time."

"I have to shower and change. Wait for me?"

"Really?"

"Yeah, really." He shakes his head and gives a confused smile. "You're here on the bleachers alone. You're here for me, right?"

"I guess. But why do you want me to stay?"

"Why not?"

"I hate that answer. People should have positive answers for things."

"I do." His voice is very quiet. "I do. You're great."

"You don't even know me."

"We've been going to school together since we were five years old."

"And the last time you talked to me before this week was six years ago."

"All right." He nods. "You're right. We went different ways . . ."

"Nuh-uh. You went a different way. I stayed where I was."

"Wow. You're angry."

"I'm not angry. Or if I am, it's not at you. Things are going on. Whatever. We're in different places now. You're the captain of the football team."

"The way you say it . . ." He drops his head. When he looks up again his eyes fix on mine. "I'm captain, Sep, not quarterback. Quarterback's the star player. I just try to hold things together. Team spirit, you know? You and me, we're not that far apart. Or we don't have to be. I don't want us to be."

He's so nice. It makes it harder somehow. I clear my throat. I have to get this out. "I want to understand what happened last night, what's happening now. I need to understand it, Joshua."

He picks up his helmet and turns, and for a second I

think he's going to walk away and tears rush to my eyes, but he's only walking in a small circle and now he's back at my foot. "This whole talking direct thing—you know, I'm trying. But it isn't as natural for me as it is for you." He clears his throat. "I don't always know the answers to what you ask. See? I'm trying, but hey." He makes a fist and taps the side of it on his lips a few times. "You're smarter than me. We both know that. We got to middle school and you got more and more serious about school, and you knew the answers, especially in science, and I . . . I don't know. I kind of forgot about you. I was glad to be busy. But then I remembered you. And now . . ." He looks away and rubs his helmet. "Now I think about you," he says slowly. "A lot."

"How come?"

He looks at me. "Come on, Sep. How am I supposed to answer a question like that?"

"Try."

He furrows his brow. "I don't know. One day, boom, there you were."

"That sounds dumb."

"Lots of things start dumb. At least in my life."

"That's not encouraging."

"Look, we're pretty different now, I get that. We've both changed—not just me—you have, too. It goes with the territory. We're different. But sometimes you've got to find out what different is like. Sometimes different can be exactly what you need." He shakes his head. "Maybe I came on too fast. Let me go shower, okay? Don't go away. Wait for me, please? Will you do that, Sep?"

"If I do, then what?"

"Then I'll take you for a ride. I've got my car here. We can drive around and talk. No parking. Just talk. Then I'll take you home. Okay?"

"Okay."

"Wait for me, Sep."

"Okay."

"Why am I afraid you'll disappear?"

I look at the back of my left hand, at the spot that hardly shows in this dark, and I slap my right hand on top of it. "I won't. I promise."

JOSHUA'S SHOWER WAS QUICK. But, then, guys are quicker than girls—or at least Dante is quicker than me. Joshua's curly hair shines wet under the parking lot lights as he opens the door for me to get into his car.

"Thanks."

He smiles, closes me in, and goes around to get into the driver's seat. "What do you feel like doing?"

"I don't know."

"All right, then, do you like water ice?"

"Sure."

We pull out and head toward Rita's Water Ice. A block away I can see the lines at every window. Maybe the whole high school decided to go to Rita's after the game. I'm pretty sure that's Sharon with her back toward us. "It'll be a long wait," I say.

"You're right." He drives on past and turns onto the pike. I can't tell if he saw Sharon. "So?"

"So?" I say back.

"If you're hungry, we can find someplace else."

"I'm not hungry." I look at him. He stops at a light and looks back at me. "But you must be."

"Nah. Not too bad. I'm just kind of wound up. I mean, I'm exhausted, but I'm still tight from all the excitement, you know? It was a good game. Now I just want to drive."

"How much gas do you have?"

"A full tank." He grins, but his eyes stay on the road. I get the feeling he's a good driver. "What time do you have to be home by?"

"I don't have a curfew."

"Really? How'd you get that lucky?"

"It never came up."

He laughs. "Tell me more."

"I never stay out very late. So it never came up."

"So would your folks worry if you didn't get home at a reasonable hour?"

"Maybe. Or maybe they wouldn't notice. They go to bed early themselves. The only one who would notice is Dante."

"Your goofy little brother—the pain." Joshua grins. "How is Squirt?"

"Big. Ninth grade."

"You want to text him, let him know?"

"It's okay to let him worry."

He laughs again. "I guess you're still not the best of friends."

"Have you become the best of friends with your sisters?"

He shrugs. "Yeah, maybe. We're close now."

"Well, Dante and I are close, I guess. But he still tries to piss me off all the time."

"How?"

"Like he calls me slut."

Joshua glances over at me quick, then back to the road. "Why?"

"Just 'cause he knows I hate it."

"Are you a slut?"

"It's a lousy word. Women need to be free from that label. I wouldn't call anyone that."

"What would you call yourself?"

The moment of truth. Or one truth, at least. "If you want to know my sexual history, you're it."

"Wow, this direct thing." He shakes his head. "Are you always so direct?"

"Why not?"

He laughs. "You stole my line."

"So it is a line?"

"No," he practically yelps. "I didn't mean it that way. I was surprised—not just at what you said, but that you'd even talk about that—and I felt, I don't know, weird, embarrassed, whatever, so I was just trying to make a joke. That's all. A lame joke. I never say anything quite right with you." He looks at me quickly with his lips pressed together and his cheeks bulge into two hard little knots. Then his eyes are back on the road. "I think maybe I'll just listen for a while."

Good. Because if he keeps talking like that—so honest and real—I may just jump him and then we'll have a major accident. "Okay."

He nods.

My mouth keeps filling with saliva. I swallow and hear my ears pop and I get the sensation of sliding, fast. I might as well finish what I started, get it over with. "I kissed a few other guys. But just kissed. It wasn't anything like last night." I remember last night so well. I've been remembering it all day. I've been tasting this boy next to me all day long. This boy who doesn't have lines and is the opposite of slick and who said I'm great. My neck feels all prickly and I wish I hadn't acted so crazy back on the bleachers, all angry, like I didn't want what I want. I wish I'd just said let's go somewhere and make out again. I wish everything didn't have to be so complicated.

Joshua turns onto the highway and heads north. We drive in silence for a long while. North, past exit after exit. Far north.

"Last night," he says at last, speaking very softly, "last night was good."

I rub both hands over my hair and down the back of my neck and leave them there, with my elbows hanging forward. I wish I could say what I want to say. My hands press against my neck hard and I want to scream. "I'm glad you're talking again. Where are we going?"

"To see Lady Liberty. If you're up for it, that is?"

I let it sink in. "The Statue of Liberty?"

"Yeah. Is that okay?"

"Where'd you get that idea?"

"You talked about women and freedom, you know, when you said how you feel about the word *slut*, and, well, I thought of her. You cool with it? 'Cause if you're not . . ."

"No no, I'm cool. It's great." I let out a whoop. "We're going to New York City!"

"Yup. You have to help me watch the signs."

"What are we looking for?"

"I'm not sure. I went with my family to Ellis Island the

summer before last—and we went from there to the statue. But late at night like this, we can't get in. The best we can aim for is a great view. And I know how to do that, if we can just make it to the southern tip of Manhattan."

"Do you have maps in the car?"

"No." He smiles at the road ahead. "I wasn't planning this. I do things with you I don't plan. You make me sort of crazy."

"You didn't plan making out last night?"

"Plan, no. Hope, yes. But only in a . . . I don't know . . . distant way. You surprised me."

You mean because I grabbed your head and kissed you all over your face? But I don't say it.

Joshua clears his throat. "I think we want to take the first tunnel we see that will get us over to Manhattan."

"All right. I'll watch for tunnels."

I am a superb navigator, but that's when we have a map. Without a map, I'm as stupid as anyone else. But I can read the word *tunnel*. And soon enough I see it and we actually pay a toll and go through a tunnel and turn south and find a parking place (my father would be popping with envy —a parking place in the city) and wind up at Whitehall Terminal.

And I finally understand. "The Staten Island Ferry."

"Yes, my lady."

The ferry comes and we're not the only ones to get on board. It's the middle of the night: 1:30 a.m., in fact. And I wish I had texted Dante, after all, but there's no point doing it now. He's asleep for sure.

We climb the stairs to the open deck on top and lean against a side rail as the ferry pulls away. The water is night black, darker than the sky by far. There are zillions of stars. I didn't know you could see so many stars so close to the city. Usually when I've been in New York City, the lights are so bright, I'm not even aware there is a sky. But tonight the sky is vast. It feels like it goes right down through the water to the end of everything.

The city is behind us now. The Statue of Liberty looms magnificent, all lit up, her chest so proud, her torch so high. And I feel it—that electric zing of patriotism that shoots through me every time I say the Pledge of Allegiance or sing the National Anthem.

The wind blows off the water and chills us. I press my arms against my sides and clutch my hands together at my waist.

"Want my jacket?" Joshua pulls his hands out of his jacket pockets and goes to take it off.

"No. No, thanks."

He puts his arm around me.

That's better.

We are tiny, tiny—infinitesimal. But not lost, far from lost. In this one blind moment, everything is perfect.

I stand on tiptoe and press my nose against the middle of Joshua's cheek.

His other arm comes around me now, too. "I thought you wanted to . . . you know . . . just talk." His voice is husky and he turns until our noses meet. "Are you changing your mind?"

I don't think my mind's part of this. I don't speak.

He touches his forehead to mine. With his arms around me so loosely, it's like we're two trees whose branches mingle at the top. "This isn't a great make-out place," he says, almost shyly.

"Just a kiss?"

"Kiss and make up, huh? Instead of kiss and make out." He gives a little chuckle. "Sorry, that was lame. Again. I get kind of self-conscious, out in public. But that's stupid. No one's looking anyway. And if they are, they can always look away. I'm ready to make up. More than ready." He breathes deep. "Lots more."

I lean into him.

We kiss. And his tongue goes in my mouth. He didn't

do that last night. We kissed so many times last night, so many ways. But he didn't do that. His tongue keeps coming in, more and more. All the way. I choke and pull back.

"Oh, I'm sorry, Sep." He gasps and shakes his head ruefully. "I guess I'm a little too ready." He rubs his mouth. "Sorry. Really. I can't believe I did that."

"It's okay." And it is. I loved the taste of him. "It was good. Till you cut off my air."

He laughs. "You're amazing."

What does he mean by that? But then, he's amazing. Everything's amazing. "Try again?"

His tongue comes in slowly this time, flickery. It's astonishing how lovely it is. I put my tongue in his mouth now. This is French kissing. I wonder how the French got to name it.

But I don't wonder long. I don't care. This is good.

19

"PUT YOUR HANDS ON the wings of the person in front of you and press." Ms. Martin walks around the outside of the circle. Her voice is soft and rhythmic.

It's Wednesday and Mamma finally agreed to let me come to Jazz Dance Club. I now have a curfew: 11 p.m. It's surprisingly fair, given how angry and frightened my parents were when I got home Sunday morning at almost 6 a.m. But I don't get to exercise that curfew for the rest of the month, because I'm grounded. Mamma went to our neighbor, Mrs. Weisskopf, for advice—she always does that—and that's what Mrs. Weisskopf recommended. I go to school and I go home, and that's it. Except that Mamma let me come here today after I played the responsibility card; I said that the rest of the club depended on me. We're all in this together. And Mamma is big on communal responsibility. It's not a total lie. We do put on one dance at the Battle of the Bands in December, after all.

It turns out Joshua had a curfew and simply broke it. So he's grounded, too. But only for a week.

"Drop your eyes so they look down toward your heart. Now slowly let your eyelids follow, until they close. Gently. But keep pressing firmly on the person in front of you."

I never noticed before how comforting Ms. Martin's voice can be. It has a low pitch for a woman, and there's a thick, mellow quality to it. She talks continually and somehow I feel like her voice supports me, physically, like it's holding my spine long and my arms just so.

We are sitting in a tight ring, one behind the other. Our legs are crossed, so I can feel the warm, smooth, wood floor under the upper part of my thighs and the outer sides of my feet. With my eyes closed, I am striving to see my heart.

If I could really look inside me now, what would I see? My mouth goes sour. If Joshua Winer could look inside me, what would he see?

Deception. I am rotten inside.

"Now move your hands to the sides of your own chest

and lift up. Lift yourself. Feel the happiness between your ribs."

There's no happiness in there. But I lift anyway. What else can I do?

Ms. Martin's still talking, always talking, and I missed what she said. But now she murmurs, "Let your hands drop easy onto your thighs. Keep sitting up tall. Let your spine stretch its full length, going down through the floor and up through the ceiling. And breathe."

She talks so much about "letting"—as though our bodies naturally want to do what she says if we'll only let them. But my hands don't fall easy, they fall like lead. My flesh feels heavy on my bones. Everything is heavy. Like just before tears come.

"Where are your palms? Are they facing up or down? Think about that. And how did you know it? With your mind or with your body?"

Someone snorts, holding in a laugh. I wonder if it's that freshman I freaked out last week. The idea of knowing with your body—that shouldn't seem laughable.

So I take Ms. Martin's question seriously. But I don't know which part of me realizes the direction my palms are facing. I can't distinguish between mind and body on some things.

But on other things it's all body. Dictator. My body is

turning me white, bit by bit. First my lips. Then the back of my hand. And this morning I found a white spot on my left breast. Shaped like a giant kidney bean. Precisely two and an eighth inches at the longest point and seven-eighths of an inch at the widest point. It's partly on the nipple. And my nipples are dark, so it shows. It glares.

I should dig a hole and crawl inside.

Instead, all I want is to be with Joshua. We sit together at lunch—or we did on Monday and Tuesday and today. He talks and I listen. Me, the big talker. I sit there and ache and want nothing more than to be close to him.

God, am I fucked.

And I don't talk that way—using that word. I don't even think that way. That's not me. That's not how my family talks. So it's bullshit to talk like that.

Or it was.

But there's no other way to say it that matches how I feel.

"We're going to take a deep breath in, then let it out and say, 'Om' all together. Holding the M as long as we can. Let the sound of light enter through the inner eye, the eye in the center of your forehead."

More snickers, from more people now. Even I wonder if Ms. Martin has gone too far. Now the class can't pay attention to whatever else Ms. Martin might say, no matter how valuable.

But I can. I will. There's something strong in Ms. Martin, and I want that strength. I don't care if she believes in inner eyes that can hear.

"Ready? Take that breath. Now, all together: *Ommmm.*"

Ommmm fills the room. *Ommmm* surrounds me. I didn't know people had that much breath.

"Open your eyelids slowly."

I open them itty bit by itty bit, not so much to follow directions as to hold back the flood I fear. I don't see why, why, goddamnit, why is this happening to me?

"You can stand now. And, Becca, it's time for you to take over."

We spread out. I avoid meeting anyone's eyes and watch as Melanie talks with Becca, then goes to put on a CD. This can be fun. It can be, really. If I just let my body do it, I can have fun. In spite of everything.

Zing! It's Usher's old song "Yeah!" I'm already bouncing on my heels, itching to fly.

And we dance. Knees coming up high, being pushed back down by our palms. Energy bouncing back and forth from right knee to left knee: bounce bounce bounce bounce bounce bounce. Our heads spin and we twirl and kick and swing so hard that the sweat drips off and stings my eyes. It feels sweet and hot. And in this moment I love my body. Take that, vitiligo. Take that! I love this body. It's strong and fast and flexible.

I shower longer and hotter than I usually do.

When I pull the curtain back, Melanie's the only one left in the locker room. She sits on the bench in her bra and dance pants with her arms halfway into a T-shirt. I'm already fully dressed when she looks up at me. That little tattoo on her ankle is of a yellow butterfly inside a pink triangle. I wonder if it's permanent. It must be; the wash-off kind, like henna, they don't last a week. Did it hurt?

"You know 'Stella Errans'?" she asks.

My cheeks go hot. She must know I was staring at her tattoo. I shake my head and lean over the sink and reapply my lipstick.

She pulls her shirt on the rest of the way. "It's a terrific song. It's from a Cirque du Soleil act called Dralion. It's great to move to."

I close my lipstick and walk in front of her toward my locker.

She smiles. "You looked good dancing today."

"Thanks." I don't know why she's being nice to me. I'm sure I wasn't so bad that someone has to feel sorry for me. "You always dance good," I say. Melanie's one of the best—so it's the truth, even though I was so caught up in moving myself I didn't notice her dancing today.

I take out a marker and touch up the three red dots on the back of my hand. One of them covers the white spot. Red is more noticeable than white, of course, but that's the point: Red looks like decoration. And one would be tacky, but three seem like some sort of pattern—the big one that's the white spot in disguise, and two satellites, like moons— so that fits with the decoration idea. I think it's working, because no one has even asked what it's all about. I smile at Melanie. "See you."

"Count on it, hottie."

What a funny thing to say. Did I dance like I was feeling sexy? I wasn't thinking about Joshua. But still, it's like Joshua lit me up anyway. The energy of passion. Whatever. It doesn't matter.

I come out and there's Owen, leaning against a wall, legs crossed at the ankles, studying his sneakers. He looks like he's loitering. "Hey, Owen."

He smiles and perks up. "Jazz dance. Oh yeah, I remember now." There's something off about the way he says it. In all the years we've been friends, I've never known Owen to bullshit, but right now I get the weird feeling that's exactly what he's doing. Was he waiting for me?

"Not just jazz dance. Yoga, too."

"Ah. Want to walk home together?"

"This is getting to be a habit," I say lightly.

"Not a bad idea," he says, as we start out. "So, what's up?"

"I could say nothing. But really there is something. And I don't want to talk about it."

He nods as though he's agreeing with himself.

"Did you just talk to yourself, Owen? Inside your head?"

"I have a rich inner life. Like Carl Jung says."

"Who's Carl Jung?"

"A big deal psychologist. Sort of like Freud. You've heard of Freud, right?"

"Cut it out, Owen. Just because you've read everything that's ever been written . . ."

"Sorry. Anyway, yeah, I talk to myself. Don't you?"

"Pretty much," I say.

"Is Joshua Winer what you don't want to talk about?"

I feel like I've been stripped naked. My little private romance—my sacred secret—has been outed. "Who told you?" And I want to kill Devin.

"You did. You told the whole school. At lunch. Three days in a row."

Of course. We're on display. And I'm so wrapped up in Joshua, I didn't even notice others watching. "Actually, that isn't what I meant when I said there was something up."

"There's something else?"

"Yeah."

"But you don't want to talk about it."

"That's right."

"Something private?"

"Mm-hmm."

"About your family? Family stuff is so—"

"Hey, let it drop. And, anyway, it's not about my family. It's just about me."

"Then I have the solution."

I look at him and blink. Owen has never been this pushy before. "The solution? Did I say it was a problem?"

"Your face did. Your face gives you away every time, Sep. Didn't you know that?"

"Fuck that."

"Yikes. Listen to Sep." He runs a few steps, slapping his feet down loudly, and I notice how really big his feet are. Out of proportion, like puppy paws. Owen's going to get a lot taller, I bet. He slows and waits for me. "You want the solution or not?"

"Yeah, okay."

"Chomsky dot info."

"What's that?"

"Noam Chomsky's website."

I know I've heard that name before, but I can't place it. "You got me again: who's Noam Chomsky?"

"The intellectual giant of our times. The guru of linguistics. The truth-monger."

I smile in spite of myself. When he gets gushy, no one's sweeter than Owen. "You like the guy."

"Go read what he has to say."

"About what?"

"Politics. The world and how it's a disaster and no one is doing anything to fix it when we could, we definitely could."

I know nothing about politics, really. I read a lot—a ton—but mostly about animals. Animals are just as complicated as humans, so that's good, but you can't get mad at them for what they do because the motivation is always straightforward—survival. "Some guru writing about politics is going to solve my problem?"

"Obviously."

"How?"

"The point is, Sep, you don't have a problem. Whatever it is, it's tiny in comparison to what a mess the world is in."

No. I have a problem. And in my life it's big. I have a right to suffer from this problem, my problem, my life. "Go away, Owen."

"Why? What did I say?"

"Just get the fuck away from me."

20

MAMMA DRIVES WITH HER hands at nine and three, exactly like our stupid Drivers' Ed. teacher last spring said we should do. Her back is straight; she always has good posture. But it's even straighter now than usual. She's holding herself together—my brave mother.

We stop at the traffic light and she turns to me with an open mouth, eyes wide, eyebrows raised.

"No!" I put up my hand. "If you say something cheerful, I'll start screaming and I won't stop."

She sighs and looks ahead again. "Well, you're healthy, at least. Every single test came out negative." She drives fast. "Dr. Ratner said he'd never seen such a perfect specimen."

"I know what he said, Mamma. I was there, too."

"Then listen to him."

"I have vitiligo, Mamma. And it's progressing. Fast. In one week I've gone from lips only, to spots on a hand, an arm, my chest, my back way down at the waist. Six. Six of them." Dr. Ratner said this happens sometimes. Zap, and you're a different person.

That's me: zapped.

"There are therapies you could try, Pina. Topical steroids, phototherapy . . ."

"You're the one who doesn't listen. None of them really work. And they all have side effects."

"Well, it's your choice, then."

"Yes. And Dr. Ratner agreed with me, if you'll remember. He said those therapies are worth trying only if you have a few small spots. You saw the size of the one on my chest. And the one on my hand is still spreading. And all the others . . . For me, it wouldn't make sense."

"It could be a lot worse, Pina."

"It will be. It's systemic. If new spots come at the rate it's been going and if they keep getting larger, I'll be a total disaster soon."

"No. I mean, you could have something a lot worse than vitiligo."

"Don't patronize me, Mamma."

"I'm just saying the truth."

"How do you know what's worse?"

"Pina! Any of those other diseases—disorders—whatever they were—any of them would have been worse."

"How do you know?"

"Because then you'd be sick. You're not sick, Pina."

"I'm a mess, Mamma. I'm a fucking train wreck."

Mamma closes her mouth and I can see her tongue pressed inside her cheek. She chews on her tongue when she's losing it. If she says something to me about my language, I really will start screaming.

"You're not a wreck," she says quietly. "You don't know whether this is it, that's all the spots you're going to get, or not. You don't know."

"Sure, Mamma. Have it your way."

She chews on her tongue some more.

"Take me to the mall again," I say.

She looks at me. "Why?"

"It can be our thing to do after visiting Dr. Ratner. We can go nine hundred times over the next year alone. Come on, Mamma. It's the least you can do."

"Don't try to manipulate me, Pina."

"Why not?"

She shakes her head. But she turns toward the mall. In minutes we're parked.

"I'll meet you back here at five thirty, okay?" I say.

"Okay."

I head for Slinky, of course. But she's not behind her counter. Some woman who looks utterly normal stands there. "Where's the usual girl?" I say. It's rude to be so abrupt, but that's me again: zapped and rude.

"Can I help you?"

"The one who works here on Thursday afternoons. On Tuesday, too. Where is that girl?"

"You must mean Carey. She's on break for"—she looks at her watch—"another ten minutes. Nine, actually."

"Where's the bathroom?"

She pulls back a little, as though offended. "Well, I don't know if she's in the bathroom . . ."

"I need to go. Fast. Can you tell me where it is? Please?"

"In the corner behind nightwear."

"Thanks." I practically run.

The bathroom is empty.

I wander through nightwear. Some for sleeping. Some for looking sexy. Lacy stuff that reveals too much.

I will never be able to wear any of this stuff. Who will want to look at my splotchy body? I pick up a sheer teddy and drop it casually on the floor and kick it under a rack of teddies.

And there's Slinky, across the aisle in the kids section looking at jeans in teeny sizes.

I race up to her. "Do you have tattoos?"

She smiles at me and nods her head. "Hello to you, too."

"Do you? On your back? Or belly maybe? Maybe around your belly button ring."

"I don't have a belly button ring. Or a tongue ring for that matter." She sticks out her tongue. "See? And I don't have tattoos." She pulls up her shirt to reveal her creamy midriff. "So what else do you want to know about me?"

She isn't bristling—she doesn't seem angry—just fed up. With that hair and stuff, people must make assumptions about her all the time. What a jerk I am.

"Sorry. I wasn't trying to pry. I'm interested in tattoos. For me."

"You?" She feigns shock.

"I wanted your advice. I'm really sorry."

"Apology accepted." She warms up. "My boyfriend has four. I know a little something about them."

"Can you make a tattoo that's natural skin color?"

"It wouldn't show, you little dingbat."

"But can you?"

"You can get a tattoo any color you can find ink in, I guess. Are you developing a lip fetish? Let me tell you, you don't want to tattoo your lips."

"Why not?"

"For one, lips are sensitive. That's why people kiss. The pain would make you crazy."

"The customer is always crazy, remember?"

She flashes a grin. "Even you aren't that crazy."

"I want a tattoo on the back of my hand."

"Well, that would hurt, too, but not as bad. Still, there are the other drawbacks."

"Like what?"

"You can have a bad reaction to the ink colors. Allergic, you know."

"They could test a little part of me first."

"Okay, sure. That makes sense. But you can get infections, too. Make sure the tattoo artist wears surgical gloves and uses disposable sterile needles. Even if you do it in someone's garage. Really."

"AIDS, you mean?"

"That, too. But I was thinking about just regular infections. Tattooing goes under the skin."

"Okay, I'll make sure."

"And then there are the diseases. Make sure you're up to date on your hepatitis and tetanus shots."

"You sound like a mom."

"I am a mom."

Right. It's hard to remember, the way she looks. "Okay, okay. I will."

"And don't just make sure, be sure."

"What do you mean?"

"Removal isn't guaranteed. Tattoos are like kids—most of them are forever. If you try to get it taken off, like with a laser, that can be painful, like really screaming painful, and it can leave a big messy scar, and it costs a ton. So be sure you want it, even when you're old and your skin sags and your fat ripples."

"You're sure the cheery one. I thought you'd be more encouraging."

"Why would you think that?"

"I don't know." My eyes sting. "I just hoped it. I just hoped you'd be different. I need encouragement."

She puts her hand on my shoulder. "You going to go all feminine and get a big yellow butterfly? Or a blue fairy?"

I think of Melanie's butterfly. It's yellow. But at least it's not big. "No."

"Good. Get a symbol. Something abstract no one else understands. Because tattoos are their own language, and if you get something common, you'll wind up sending messages you don't want to send." She shoots a teasing smile at me and wags her finger in the no-no gesture. "You could wind up a member of a gang."

I slap my hands on my throat and look aghast.

"Laugh, but it's true. Whatever. Draw the symbol yourself and ask the tattoo artist to copy it. There are great Celtic symbols on the Internet. You could get ideas from them."

"Are you Irish?"

"My dad is."

I look at my watch. "How long does it take?"

"A tattoo? How big do you want it?"

I look at the spot on my hand. It's bigger all the time. "The whole back of my hand."

"Maybe an hour with an experienced tattoo artist. I don't think much more."

"Then I can't do it by five thirty. That's only ten minutes away."

"Ack! It's already five twenty? I've got to get back to the cosmetics counter."

I trail behind her.

The woman who was covering for her leaves with a thin smile and not a single word.

"Do you like her?" I ask.

"She's okay. I don't really know her."

"Should I get the tattoo? Should I cover my body in tattoos?"

"I don't know you, either. I don't know if you should get a tattoo. But I'm almost sure you shouldn't cover your body in them."

"Why not? Look at you. Look at your hair and your nails. You decorate yourself. Why shouldn't I?"

"Hair and nails are dead. But your skin is alive. Live things have a dignity. They demand respect."

"What about your boyfriend?"

"What about him? He makes up his own mind. I don't like his tattoos. He likes them. He does it for himself. I like ordinary skin."

"I don't have ordinary skin."

"It looks ordinary to me."

"You haven't seen all of it."

"Whatever kind of skin you have, it's better than a tattoo. It's alive. It's good. Love it."

"Not everything alive is good."

"You're right. But you got to love them anyway."

"Like Jesus would?"

"Why not? Any other choice sucks."

Sometimes religious people do make sense.

21

"MAMMA!" I RUN THROUGH the house looking for her. And there she is, on her knees, straightening the books in Dad's study. They don't need straightening. I can see by her cheek that she's chewing on her tongue.

"What is it, Pina?" She sits back on her heels and studies the bookshelf as though it matters. And it dawns on me: having something go wrong for her child mystifies her. She's helpless, and Mamma hates being helpless. I feel sorry for her, which surprises me, because feeling sorry for myself just about saturates me—there's hardly room for anyone else.

"I'm taking Rattle for a walk."

That makes her head turn toward me. "You never take Rattle for a walk without being asked."

"I'm a new girl, remember?"

"Not that new." She stands and leans over to rub the back of her knees. "It's Friday afternoon and you just got home from school. This is collapse time for you."

"So what? I want to take Rattle for a walk."

"You're not planning on meeting up with that Joshua, are you?"

"He's just Joshua. Not 'that Joshua.' You know him, Mamma. You've known him forever. And he came over and apologized. What more do you want? Anyway, no. He has an away football game tonight. He couldn't see me even if I broke your rules and ran off with him for the night. And I wouldn't run off, anyway. You know that."

"Do I? You're a new girl."

"Not that new."

She gives a sad smile. "Okay, thanks. Rattle will enjoy it. He can still smell everything, at least. Don't let him eat anything gross."

"I know his habits, Mamma. I love him. I'll keep him on a short leash."

I go into the living room. Rattle's asleep on Nonno's old chair. I pet his head tenderly. "Hey, old boy. Wake up. Let's go for a walk."

He opens his bleary eyes and turns his big head to me. And I wonder if most blind people walk around with their eyes open behind their dark glasses. Or do they close them to keep out dirt and stuff? I've known blind kids. But I never thought to ask. Which is good, I guess. I mean, it would seem rude to ask something like that, it could hurt someone's feelings, though it shouldn't. But should doesn't matter when it comes to feelings.

I might flip out if someone saw me in the shower and asked about my breast.

"Come on, Rattle."

He drops his head back on his paws and closes his eyes again. Does he see anything?

I stare at him, trying to detect movement under those eyelids—a hint of what might be going on—when, zap, the idea comes. This is nine hundred times better than what I'd been planning.

I take the stairs as fast as I can and open my laptop and search Google. There it is: *Om*. The sound of light in Hindu scriptures. To one side of the explanation is the symbol for the sound. To the other side is a statue of the Buddha with that dot on the forehead, the third eye, the door to inner perception, through which the sound of light can penetrate.

I don't understand the inner eye and my intellect rebels against it. But Ms. Martin seems transported when she speaks to us about it during the asanas. Is she a blissed-out mystic?

I am not a mystic. I love eating steak. I love getting filthy just so I can wash off and feel squeaky clean again. I love cutting my hair and being surprised at the new me. I love kissing Joshua. God, do I love kissing Joshua. I'm as far from a mystic as anyone can be.

But I need a tattoo. And if anyone asks what it is, I can make up things that will make their jaw drop. I stifle a laugh. Dante's in the next room, and I don't want him hearing me laugh to myself.

I take the sheet of paper out of my pocket and unfold it. There's the Celtic symbol I chose off the Internet last night. It's complex: a mandala in its own right. But the symbol for *Om* is better. It can sit on a white background and no one will even know that the color of the background isn't on purpose.

I draw the best *Om* I can on the back of the sheet and put it in my pocket. Then I race down the stairs and lean over Rattle in Nonno's chair. "I'll let you smell garbage cans," I whisper in his ear. "We can walk by the college fraternities and you can smell the vomit out back."

He snuffles in his sleep.

"All right, we'll go by the sororities and I'll let you smell the tampons." That's Rattle's most perverse delight.

He opens those eyes and actually gets off the chair. Does he really know the word *tampon*?

We go straight to Devin's house. I deceived my dog, but what could I do? I'll make it up to him later.

I see Devin watching for me through her living room window. She waves and comes out as Rattle and I amble up to the door. "I'm not going to do it, Sep."

I nod. "I figured you might back out. It's okay. You don't need to look exotic—you're not damaged."

She winces. "Don't you do it, either."

"Aw, Devin, I already made up my mind." I take the paper out of my pocket and hold it out to her. "See? Isn't it nice?"

"Is that Om?"

I'm crestfallen. "How do you know about Om?"

"Everybody knows about Om."

"Oh. Well, it's perfect. Don't you think it's perfect?"

She takes the paper from me. "For a Hindu."

"Buddhists, too."

"You're not Buddhist, Sep." She turns it over. "What's this other thing? I like it."

"That's Celtic. It's a mandala."

"What's a mandala?"

"Something you can look at for a long time, and the

more you look at it, the more you see. It allows you to meditate."

Devin gives the paper back to me. "I'd do it with you, Sep, I really would. Only this afternoon I read something important. So we can't."

"What did you read?"

"Tattoos should be kept out of the sun. Or covered with major sunscreen, like SPF forty-five or higher. Otherwise you might get a melanoma there. A skin cancer."

Her words are making me dizzy. "I know what melanoma is, Devin."

She shakes her head. "So don't, Sep. You told me that the white spots are already super susceptible to cancer. You can't do something that makes them even more susceptible."

"I'll wear gloves."

"Like a ghoul? Everyone will think you're Dracula. And that will cause a lot more attention than white spots."

I glare at her.

"Okay, I take that back. That was a stupid thing to say. But if you're going to go around with gloves anyway, then why get a tattoo?"

"For when I take the gloves off, Devin." And tears come tumbling down my fat cheeks. I drop the leash and press the heels of my hands against my closed eyelids. Tattoos were my last chance. My only way to hide. My only way to keep things going with Joshua. Now there's nothing.

And then Devin's holding me, all warm and tight, and I'm crying harder. "Come on inside, Sep."

I feel like I'm melting, nothing but bodily effluents, the things people flush away fast.

I shake her off and wipe at the tears. "Your mom doesn't let Rattle in the house, remember?"

"She's not home."

"She'll smell he was here and she'll have an allergic reaction and you'll be in trouble."

"Shut up and come in, Sep."

We go inside to her bedroom. Rattle sniffs everything, then collapses in a heap and falls asleep.

"Tattoos were a dumb idea, anyway, even if our fake IDs had worked." Devin sits on her bed.

I plop down beside her.

"If this vitiligo thing really does keep going, what were you planning on doing—getting more and more tattoos?"

I imagine myself with nine hundred tattoos. "God, am I an idiot."

"No you're not. You're the smartest person I know. You just can't think straight about this whole thing. No one could. Anyway, I went on the Internet. There's a site that shows people who got tattoos years ago. Sep, they look really bad when you're old."

"You sound like Slinky," I say.

"Who's Slinky?"

"A girl who works in the department store. She's become my mentor in life."

"Oh yeah? How come?"

"I don't know. I have the feeling she's figured things out. Totally juicy."

"You'll figure things out, Sep. You always do."

"I can't! It doesn't matter what my head does. It's this goddamned body of mine."

"Stop with the cursing, okay?"

I pull back and stare at her face. What a jerk I am. My best friend. The only one outside my family I'm honest with these days. I don't want to offend her. And if I don't want to be alone the rest of my life, I better shape up. People like me—defective people—we have to be nice, nicer than most others.

"I'm sorry, Devin."

"I know. It's okay."

"Nothing's okay. I'm afflicted. Like in medieval times. A curse has descended on my head."

"See? I told you you were still Catholic. You always say

you're not. But only a Catholic would talk like that. Or maybe a Jew. Rachel talks like that sometimes. You're Catholic, Sep. You can take the girl out of the church, but you can't take the church out of the girl."

I laugh. "Who told you that?"

"It's a variation on something my father says."

"You're so smart."

"And you're surprised, aren't you?" She looks at me slyly.

"I'm sorry if I treated you like a dumbo."

"You don't have to keep apologizing. You're not a pariah yet."

I blink. "You really are brilliant."

I go home to cook Rattle a hamburger. After all, right is right. Plus I pop a vitamin pill. That's part of my new regimen—it has all the vitamins and minerals a vitiligo victim needs.

In the middle of flipping the burger I remember that I didn't even ask Devin what's up with Charlie. All we talk about anymore is what's up with me.

I'm an egotistical pig.

And I can't blame that on vitiligo.

22

SLINKY WAS RIGHT AND Slinky was wrong. Hair and nails don't have feeling in them, so maybe that's why she classifies them as not alive. But they grow.

Take a hair shaft on a horse, for example. Under the skin, at the base of the shaft, there are two follicles. One is a growth follicle and the other is a color-producing follicle —which, of course, is the one I care about. Both are alive.

A popular way of branding horses is by freezing. You put a bitterly cold iron on the horse's skin, which is covered with hair, and hold it there for the right amount of time with the right amount of pressure. The color-producing follicles will die. So when new hair grows, it will be pure white.

On the other hand, if you press the freezing iron there too long or too hard, the growth follicles will die, too, and you'll have a bald brand.

I stare at my own skin. Skin is more complicated than hair. It turns out that our skin is a single organ. The body's heaviest organ. It has an upper layer, the epidermis, which looks smooth to the eye, but, in fact, is a bunch of hills and valleys. Its main function is to protect what's under it. And it has a lower layer, the dermis.

Tattoo ink is injected between the epidermis and the dermis. But that's not my concern anymore; I'm not getting tattoos. I'm reading about skin because my skin is my enemy right now. And what's the old saying: Know thy enemy.

Below the dermis is a fatty layer. Under that are arteries and veins and nerves.

In most mammals the fatty layer is connected firmly to the skin. But not in all. So you can skin a rabbit easily, because the skin splits off like a jacket. You can't do that to a mouse or a guinea pig. Or a human.

Okay. That's a good thing about my skin. I can appreciate that.

Below the fatty layer is a sheet of muscle called the *panniculus carnosus*. In humans it covers the jaw and parts of the face. But in most mammals it runs all over the head and torso and halfway down the limbs. So a horse can twitch its flank when a fly lands on it, but people can't. We can twitch the skin on our jaw, though. And make funny faces. Without the *panniculous carnosus*, our faces would be deadpan.

Okay. I'm grateful for my *panniculous carnosus*. I like my expressive face.

All right, Slinky, all right, all right. I love my skin, my lifesaving enemy. I have to. Like you say, any other choice sucks.

I close my computer as my phone beeps. A message from Joshua: "u there? talk to me."

It's Saturday, and only 9 a.m. I type: "ur awake early!"

"went 2 bed early. Grounded. Remember?"

"u won last nite. congrats."

"thnx. 2 bad u weren't there. I missed u."

I type: "me 2."

His answer is immediate: "still on for 2nite?"

My pulse speeds. I'm not good at sneaking. I never had to do it before. I let out my breath noisily. I can't afford a month of being grounded: I'm like a fruit about to pass from ripe to rotting. I have to stay in continual motion. Never in my life have I understood a swift or a tuna better. Time is running out—it's now or never.

I type: "yes."

"time?"

I'm babysitting for Sarah again. Mrs. Harrison almost cried with gratitude when I called her on Tuesday and said I could sit for her Saturday if she wanted. It was sort of Joshua's idea, and sort of mine. We came up with it at lunch that day at the same moment.

I type: "they leave at 7. how about 8?"

"7:05."

I laugh. Joshua acts like he's the one with vitiligo. "What if they linger? 7:15."

"7:10."

I close the computer and go downstairs to do my homework. I like to work at the kitchen table.

Dad's drinking coffee, probably his nine hundredth this morning, and looking out the back window.

"What's up?" I ask.

"A fox."

"Really?" I run to the window, but all I see is the bushes and trees at the rear of our yard. "Where?"

"He went by around seven."

"Dad! That was hours ago."

"I know. I come back every so often to look at where he went. He was big, with a huge tail—a real fox tail."

"That's what foxes have, Dad."

He keeps looking out back.

So I do, too.

There are still tomatoes in Mamma's little garden plot. They stand with brown leaves in their cone-shaped cages. In August we had a ripe armload every day. But now the few left are green.

A female cardinal alights on a tomato cage. A male watches her from the spruce. She moves her tail up and down, up and down. Is she doing it on purpose to drive that male crazy? Do males go crazy when it isn't mating season?

"I've got more spots, Dad," I say in the most level voice I can manage. My fingers grip the edge of the counter and turn white. But that's bloodless white, not vitiligo white.

"You'll always be beautiful, Pina."

"Don't say that. I can't bear it when you say that. You have no idea what it means."

"I have to say what I think."

"But it doesn't matter what you think. Can't you see that, Dad?"

"It always matters what the people we love think."

"I'm going to see Joshua tonight." It came out—it just came out, like a hiccup or a sneeze.

He puts his coffee cup on the counter and folds his arms across his chest. But he's still looking out the window. "You're grounded for a month, aren't you? This is only the beginning of that month."

"I'm babysitting. He's coming to help me."

"Help you? Is that what you call it?"

"Yes, Dad. That's exactly what I call it."

He puts his whole hand over his mouth and slides it down to his chin, as if he's rubbing away all the things he might have said. "Well, we get help where we can. Just don't be foolish, Pina."

"When have I ever been foolish, Dad?"

"Last weekend. Saturday night was pretty damn foolish."

I kiss him on the cheek. "If that's the only example you can think of, wouldn't you say it's about time?"

"Maybe that's what it feels like to you, Pina. But foolish isn't nearly as good as it's cracked up to be."

23

"OH, SEP, IS THAT YOU?"

I look up in surprise. "Hey, Ms. Martin." She's walking a huge white dog with hair in clumps like dirty clouds. "I didn't know you lived around here."

"I don't. Or not that close anyway. But it's Saturday, and Monster likes a good long walk on Saturday."

I smile. "Her name is Monster?"

"It's a he, actually. His real name is Mandar. It's a good Hindu name for a male dog. But my niece dubbed him Monster. She was only four when I got him, and *Mandar* sounded like *monster* to her, I guess. Anyway, it stuck."

Monster sniffs at my hand.

I scratch his big head, and wonder what he can feel through all that fur. Under it, his skin is pink for sure. Most dogs have pink skin regardless of the color of their fur. But dogs with black fur have skin in charcoal hues. And Dalmatians have pink skin with dark spots where the black fur grows. And if I keep thinking about skin, I may start slobbering like some halfwit.

"He likes you, Sep. Usually he's diffident with strangers."

"Probably he just smells my dog." I straighten up. "Are you Hindu?"

"No. But I like Hindu things." She pulls a chain out from inside her shirt. A fat yellow man with an elephant head hangs from it. "Do you know who this is?"

"Some god, right?"

"Lord Ganesh, in fact. Feel. Real ivory."

It's cool and smooth and seems almost soft. "Isn't ivory white?"

"This is old. Real ivory yellows." She slips it back inside and pats her shirt. "Ganesh removes all obstacles."

I shake my head, holding in a laugh. "That's a good trick."

"Among the best." Ms. Martin looks at me intensely, as though she's about to say something important. It makes me nervous.

"I better keep going or I'll be late to my babysitting job."

"All right, Sep. See you Wednesday. You're doing very well in dance club this year, you know. You have more of a sense of your body. It's good to see that kind of real understanding. You're becoming a warrior."

I can't help but blink.

She smiles. "You don't remember when I talked about warriors, do you?"

My neck goes hot. "I know the warrior poses, but that's all. I'm sorry."

"That's okay. I'm sure you were attending to something else equally important when I was talking about them." She pats Ganesh through her shirt again. "If you build endurance in sustaining a warrior pose, you'll be able to stand up for yourself, to argue without fear, to refuse without apology. Those are qualities of a warrior. That's what I see developing in you, Sep."

"Thank you, Ms. Martin." I'm flushing with embarrassment. I look down and hurry on.

I feel weird about her saying I'm becoming a warrior. But she's right: I do have more of a sense of my body now. And it's getting stronger. Maybe that's because it's betraying me.

The front light is not on at the Harrisons' house. They haven't adjusted to September yet. Evening falls earlier every day. Somehow Mrs. Harrison is always behind.

Maybe she wants time to stop and wait till she's ready for it. I can understand that. I don't think it's going to work out for her—or me—but, hey, I can understand it.

I ring the bell. Mr. Harrison answers. Mr. Harrison never answers.

"Hello . . . Sep."

I can see from his eyes that he's relieved he remembered my name. How can it be so hard for him? I'm the only steady babysitter they have. Anyone else is a once-is-enough sitter.

I walk in past him and Sarah comes flying across the room and tackles my shins.

"Football!" she screams.

I look down at her and am tempted to clap a hand over her mouth before she can say what I'm almost sure is coming next.

"Football?" says Mrs. Harrison, straightening her pearls as she comes into the room. "Girls don't play football."

"Joshua does!" screams Sarah. I knew it. Damn. "So I do, too." She hugs me harder.

I struggle to keep my balance.

"Who's Joshua?" asks Mrs. Harrison with a frown. "There aren't any Joshuas in your nursery class."

"He's Sep's Joshua."

Mrs. Harrison looks at me.

"He's a friend," I say. "He came over last Friday while I was sitting. Do you mind?"

Mrs. Harrison's lips part.

"No." Mr. Harrison steps forward abruptly and takes Mrs. Harrison by the elbow. "You can have a friend over, Sep. Let's go, Amy."

Mrs. Harrison nods frantically. "Of course. Have fun."

"You have fun," I call, sincerely.

But they're already gone. Like escapees.

I laugh.

Sarah lets go and stands in front of me. "What's funny?"

"Your parents."

She smiles. "Funny parents. Funny funny parents." She runs once around me then straight to the couch. "Want—to—play—with—Le—gos?" Each syllable comes between jumps.

It is a springy couch. I remember it well.

"Sure."

She sails off the couch and lands with a splatter, barely missing the coffee table. It's a wonder that Sarah has made it alive this long. But in seconds she's up off the floor without a tear and dumping the Legos in a heap.

The doorbell rings.

Sarah looks at me with a big O mouth.

I nod.

She runs for the door and opens it with a loud, "Hello, Joshua!"

"Hi, Boss."

"I'm Sarah."

"Hi, Sport."

"I'm Sarah."

"Hi, Sarah!"

"Yay!" Sarah grabs his hand and pulls him into the house.

I shut the door behind him.

"Want to play Legos or football?" asks Sarah. "You choose. You're the guest. Choose." She runs for the couch and jumps again. "Choose—choose—choose."

I've seen Sarah hyper before. A lot. But this is extreme even for her. I swear it feels like sexual energy, because if I let myself, I could be jumping on that couch right beside her. How young do girls start feeling the thrill of sexuality?

"I'm kind of tired. How about you do Legos and I'll sit on the couch and watch?"

Sarah lands from a jump onto her bottom. Then she scoots off the couch. "Okay. It's yours. Sit."

"Okay, Boss."

Sarah giggles.

"I mean Sport."

Sarah laughs.

"I mean Sarah." Joshua sits on the couch.

Sarah goes to the Lego pile and sits demurely by it. "Come on, Sep. Let's build. For Joshua." This child is definitely flirting.

I sit across the pile from Sarah and we build.

"What are you making?" asks Joshua, after a while.

"Everything," says Sarah. "See?" She holds up her creation.

"And you, Sep?"

I smile sheepishly. "I'm just putting together pieces at random."

"That's how I feel about building. I'm supposed to be building right now. It's a stupid physics project on keystones, but I haven't even started yet and it's due Monday." He leans forward and puts his elbows on his knees and wrings his hands. "Between practice after school every day and games on the weekends—I don't know. I'm already behind. I wish I'd never taken physics."

"What's physics?" asks Sarah.

"Everything," says Joshua. "Or, rather, everything is physics. That's what my teacher says."

"What's keystones?"

I'm amazed that she remembers the word. She's smart.

"They're the stone in the middle of an arch that gives the whole thing stability. Without the keystone, the arch would fall apart."

"Do you know what an arch is?" I ask Sarah.

"Everybody knows. A rainbow is an arch."

"That's right," I say. "You're smart, Sarah. But rainbows aren't built by people. When people build arches from blocks of stone, they need something to hold it all together. The keystone does that. It's at the very top, in the center."

"Glue is good."

"Right again," I say. "But that's cheating. On this project at least." I look over at Joshua and tilt my head in question.

He nods. "No glue. Definitely no glue."

I turn back to Sarah. "If you cut the stones right and have a keystone, pressure alone can hold it firm."

"Use Legos." Sarah scoops up a handful and holds them out toward Joshua.

"Legos have those little bumps that hold them together. That's sort of like glue."

"Cheating is bad," says Sarah. She drops the Legos on the floor again.

"So what are you going to do?" I ask Joshua.

"I don't know. I guess tomorrow I'll try to find some sort of cube—maybe Styrofoam or something—and shave it to make the curving parts and whatever. It's a big pain.

Mrs. Spinelli is treating us like fourth graders, as though we won't get the concept unless we do it with our own hands."

"I'm four," says Sarah.

"'Fourth graders' doesn't mean they're four years old," I say. "It means—"

"But I'm four," interrupts Sarah. "After Halloween, I'll be five. Now I'm four." She stares at me.

I stare back. "I'm sixteen," I say.

"So am I," says Joshua.

"I agree with Mrs. Spinelli," I say. "I think it's good to learn with your body—your hands. It's different from just learning with your head. And you're a hands guy anyway. You play football. You've got physics in your body every time you throw or catch that ball."

He smiles. "If you start up that road, you'll say dogs can do physics. They run and catch Frisbees, after all."

"Not Rattle," I say.

"Rattle." He smiles and shakes his head. "How is the pup?"

"Practically blind."

"I'm sorry."

"Don't be. It's just because he's so old now. He's a tam . . . He's a happy garbage guy."

"Like I'm a happy 'hands guy'?"

I smile. "Anyway, don't begrudge Mrs. Spinelli's wanting you to build an arch."

"With a keystone, don't forget. This is Pennsylvania, the Keystone State."

"We have sweet potatoes," says Sarah.

"Sweet potatoes?" Joshua gives a lopsided smile.

"You can make anything with sweet potatoes. Mommy says. Soup, pie, bread." Sarah marches into the kitchen and comes back with three big sweet potatoes. Joshua and I look at each other and smile. We chop them into cubes.

A half hour later an orange arch stands about eight inches high on a pane of glass from one of the old photo frames in Sarah's garage. That way Mrs. Spinelli will be able to look at it from underneath and see every part. That was Sarah's idea, too.

Sarah might be brilliant. Sarah and Devin. Brilliant people.

We bathe Sarah and she sits between Joshua and me on her bed. He offered her his lap, but she got shy and nestled closer against me. He reads aloud. Three books. Like always.

Then we both kiss her good night.

And we go back into the living room.

We stand a moment, silent. Then Joshua takes me in

his arms and holds me close, and we kiss. He maneuvers us to the couch.

"Lights out," I say quickly. Evil deceiver that I've become. I've been thinking about this all day, all week. The fact that I should tell Joshua about my vitiligo just sits there like a festering wound hidden under a lacy shawl. But I have no intention of exposing it—I refuse to think why, sometimes a person has a right not to think—so my job is to keep him from lifting the lace. I need the safety of the dark. "Lights out, first."

"How come?"

"It's my way of having a Ganesh necklace."

"What's a Ganesh necklace?"

"A Hindu god that hangs around your neck and removes all obstacles."

"You know, half the time with you I have no idea what's going on. But I'm game." Joshua gets up and turns off the overhead light. Then he turns off the lamp by the chair, too.

"It's completely dark," I say.

"Wait a moment." Joshua stands still. "Can you see my silhouette now?"

"Yes."

"I can see yours, too. And even in the dark you're beautiful."

He couldn't have said anything worse. I can't do this. In an instant I'm all new resolve. "Will you sit with me and talk?"

"Sure." He comes and sits beside me. He doesn't touch me, not even with his leg.

"I'm not beautiful."

"Isn't that a subjective matter?"

I try again. "I almost got a tattoo yesterday." It seems like so long ago—but it was just yesterday.

I hear him suck in air. "Is this a . . . I don't know . . . some kind of confession or something?"

"Sort of."

He's silent. Finally, he says, "You sure didn't act like that last weekend." His voice is quiet and sad.

"Like what?"

"Like what you're telling me."

"What do you think I'm telling you?"

"What are you telling me?"

"That I almost got a tattoo to hide behind."

"Oh." He gives a little laugh. "I thought you were saying you were lesbian."

"What?" I give a laugh. "Why would you think that?"

"Some of the lesbians at school started that last year. Didn't you know? They got pink triangles on their ankles, with junky little things inside."

I wonder if Melanie's a lesbian. "I didn't know. No."

"I mean, I don't care. I've got nothing against lesbians." He laughs. "They like doing a lot of the same things I like doing, after all. I just don't want you being one."

"I'm not."

"Good. That's very good."

I should tell him. I was just about to. And this is the right time. I should tell him. It's ridiculous not to.

But it will be too brief as it is. I won't make it briefer. I can't. Even if he hates me later. Even if I hate myself. I want to have Joshua as a boyfriend for however long I can.

Silence hums in the air.

"I don't like tattoos much," whispers Joshua. "In fact, they give me the chills. My grandmother had a long number tattooed on her arm. She was in Auschwitz when she was a little girl. I used to stare at that number when I'd sit on her lap, but I was afraid to touch it." He breathes really hard. "But if you got one, I'd do my best to learn to love it."

I can't speak. I blink back tears.

Silence again.

Finally, Joshua lets out a long sigh. He takes my hand. "I want to hold you, Sep. I want to kiss you. I want to . . . I want to do whatever you want to do. I want to know you."

I bring his hand up in front of me and press my face into it.

And we lie down and kiss. Slow and then fast and everything soft and hard. Like Ovid's idea of the creation, a whirl of everything, a universe emerging from chaos. Only I don't feel like I'm coming together. I feel like I'm coming apart. Falling into nine hundred little pieces. Like snowflakes. How far can you fall into a kiss?

Joshua rolls so I'm on top. His hands go up and down my back. Those big, wide hands. They press my ribcage. And I remember Ms. Martin making us lift up our own ribcages, telling us to feel the happiness inside. Right now there is happiness inside me. Joshua's hands give me happiness, they become my happiness. Up and down, never straying toward my sides, so firmly up and down. Up and down till I'm almost crazy, begging him inside my head.

And then they tug at my shirt. They pull it up. Slowly. Agonizingly slowly. But steady. This is happening. It's real. Maybe there is a Lord in heaven.

I straddle his waist and lift my arms up high and my shirt comes off over my head. He sits partway up and kisses my neck and throat and the hollows above and below my collarbone. He kisses at the top of my breasts. And his hands fumble with my bra clasps, but only for a second. My bra slips down my arms. He untangles it from my wrists and cups my breasts with both hands. I gasp at how good it feels.

I am here.

Colors don't show in the dark. And you can't feel them. Colors don't matter now. My breasts feel as good as anyone's. I am as good as anyone. In this moment I am worthy of him.

And it isn't unfair to Joshua. He's doing what he wants to do. He's a hands guy, a happy hands guy. I'm not hurting him. Please. I can't be hurting him.

We are kissing and his hands keep stroking me. It just keeps getting better. And now, at last, his head moves toward me. I can feel the wet heat as he opens his mouth.

This is the meaning of *exquisite*.

24

I AM STANDING BESIDE my bed in the second warrior pose. I have been practicing this pose on and off all morning—to the right, then to the left, equal amounts of time on both sides. It takes strength. My arms ache. My thighs shake. But being a warrior is worth it.

At first I just counted in my head, to make sure I was holding the pose the same amount of time on both sides. Symmetry matters. It's part of balance—and balance is part of harmony and harmony is good. I want good. But now I have a feel for how much time has passed. So I just hold the pose without counting.

Mr. Dupris has filled my head with archaea. If any living creatures are true warriors, it's archaea. So it's right that they should fill my head while I do this pose. I don't think I ever even heard of them before this year. Tiny, one-celled creatures, similar to bacteria, they're everywhere. Some archaea are found at the North Pole in temperatures that go down to minus eighty-five degrees Celsius and never go above freezing. Or, at least, never used to, before global warming. Some archaea live at the bottom of the sea, miles below the surface, near places where heat from the earth's core spews out, so that the water temperature goes up to one hundred and ten degrees Celsius. That's more than boiling—but the pressure down there keeps the water liquid. Some archaea live in salt and some live in acid. They are tough warriors, strong in accepting their own worth and the worth of the world. Because the two are the same. We are all the same, we are all part of everything. That's what Ms. Martin says.

I change to the left side: right leg straight, left leg bent now. I hold the pose and line up my body parts correctly and look over my left arm. Slowly my ears buzz with a high-pitched *E* and I don't feel anything in my legs really, or even my arms. Tension leaves, dissipates just like that, and I feel like I could stand here forever. I want to. I'm floaty, free of worry.

I come out of the pose and stand tall like a mountain, and let what just happened to me sink in. I'm lucky. Me, the girl with vitiligo. I can be a warrior, if I let myself. I can move beyond into someplace where I'm strong.

I climb on my bed and cross my legs and sit quietly. The way I felt a moment ago is gone. Like rain ceasing in an instant. It's a disappointment. I'm Sep again, the screwed-up girl who's lying to her boyfriend and who feels sorry for herself in the process.

The funny thing is, when I'm actually with Joshua, when we're all tangled together, I feel like I did in the warrior pose. Like I could do it forever. Like nothing else is pressing on me, nothing else matters.

This morning I finished reading a sex novel. It's my third. And two other novels with sex in them are under my pillow. I borrowed them from Devin. The way things progress in them is predictable. As though there's an order to sex—first you do X, then Y, then Z. I wanted to know. But now I don't like it. What happens between Joshua and me is too good to be formulaic. And I don't like how the girl just waits for the guy to make all the moves. He's the leader, she's the follower. I won't read the other two—I'll give them back to Devin.

It dawns on me that Devin had these novels. And read them. Is she sleeping with Charlie? So fast? But she would have told me. Only maybe I never gave her the chance.

Mamma comes into my room. Silently. She stands by my bureau and looks at me. And I was just thinking of sex novels and Devin's possibly racy sex life. Can she see it in my face?

"I'm waiting." She puts her fists on her hips, arms akimbo. For other people that would be hostile. For Mamma it's just the way she waits. She doesn't look hostile. In fact, she looks vulnerable.

"I don't have anything to tell you, Mamma."

"Yes you do."

And suddenly I know: "Dad told you Joshua came over to babysit with me last night."

"Yes."

"He can't keep a secret."

"If it was a secret, why did you tell him?"

She's right, of course. "So you know. So don't ask."

"Pina, it's like I don't even know you. In a matter of days, you're someone new. What's gotten into you?"

"I'm sixteen, Mamma. Isn't that what adolescence is supposed to be all about?"

"I don't think it's that simple."

"What ever is?"

"Don't get smart with me, Pina. Talk to me, please. Tell me about Joshua."

"You know him."

"I knew him. I don't know him now. Is he nice?"

"He's very nice."

"Do you know how to . . ."

"I'm learning."

"What I want to say—what worries me—is do you know how to be careful?"

"You mean birth control?"

"Has it come to that?"

"It's not your business whether it has or not."

"It is my business whether you're safe, Pina."

"Who's ever safe, Mamma?"

"I hate this thing you do now, this answering me with questions. They aren't even good questions. Some of us are safe, some of the time. Safe from doing something dangerous."

"What's not dangerous, Mamma?"

"I will slap you if you keep that up."

I can't remember when Mamma last slapped me. "I'm sorry." And now I really am. She's just trying to be a good mother. "If I need birth control, I'll get it."

"It isn't just that. It's who you are. What are you trying to prove?"

Oh, no. This is not the direction I'm going to allow us to go. No. "I have homework."

"I think we should talk about your vitiligo. Dr. Ratner says it's important to talk about it."

I push up my sleeve so she can see the new spot on my elbow. It looks like a big splash of grease cooled and congealed into white slop. "That won't make it go away."

Mamma looks at my elbow and blinks. "Of course not." Now she looks at my face. "But it may make it less frightening to you."

"How? Come on, Mamma. Get real. I wish I had Daddy's coloring so it wouldn't show so bad. Instead, I'm even darker than you. And you know what else, you want to know what else I wish sometimes?" I clench my teeth.

She blinks again.

"I wish Devin had gotten it instead of me. She's so much lighter than I am. It wouldn't be as bad for her. And then I hate myself for wishing that. Vitiligo is hideous for everyone." I feel a tear rolling down my cheek. Then a flood. "I love Devin, and I still wish it sometimes."

Mamma rushes to the bed and holds me and rocks me and I'm crying so hard that I'm unable to catch my breath.

I fight her, push at her. But she keeps holding me, rocking me, and we're both sobbing now.

"You need to refocus, Pina." She smooths my hair away from my forehead, over and over.

"Don't tell me there's good ahead. Devin said that the other day and I thought of stabbing her."

"I don't mean ahead. I mean now. You need to look at now, and what is good. You need to focus on what is good now."

"That's what I'm trying to do, Mamma. Joshua's good."

"Does he know?" She doesn't have to add what about.

"No."

She pushes me back so she can look in my face. "How good could he be, if you don't trust him enough to tell him?"

"It's my fault I don't trust him. Not his."

"You're making things more difficult than they have to be, Pina."

"I don't think so, Mamma. I think this is how they have to be." I bury my head against her again. "Mamma?" I whisper.

"What, baby?"

"I used to be normal." I'm breathing now, but it hurts—it hurts like a frozen spike in my sternum. "I'll never be normal again. It's spread on my chest. And belly. And I know it will be all over my face soon. I know it. And there's nothing I can do about it—no amount of being good or following rules or anything else can save me." All I can manage is a whisper. "You saw the photos in those medical books. Strangers will do double takes on the street. Nice people will look away to not be rude."

"Maybe strangers. But others will adjust."

"How will I ever even have a successful job interview?"

She hugs me hard. "You'll go to a top college and have whatever jobs you want. You're the best student in your class."

"That's not true. Owen is."

"That's your opinion."

I squeeze her arm. "Who will ever love me?"

"Anyone who knows you."

"But I won't be me anymore. I'm not even me now."

"You're you, Giuseppina." She kisses me as soft as air. "You'll always be you."

Maybe that's the real problem. Because I hate me—liar me.

25

I CLOSE JOHN STEINBECK'S novel *The Red Pony*. The first part of it haunts me. The boy's pony gets sick just from being out in the rain, and winds up dying. What kind of animal dies because of rain? Why does nature screw up so much?

I open my calculus homework for the second time and stare again at the sentence that made me stop last time: *A logarithmic function is the inverse of an exponential function.* I reread it three more times, and I'm still not sure what it means. And I'm good at math.

But maybe I'm not as good as I think. And I'm in a

rush—I've got plans. I swallow my pride and text Owen: "hey, Owen. u there?"

"ur alive! and talking to me! will wonders never cease?"

And I realize, I haven't heard from him since I was so mean. Six days without hearing from Owen—I think that's the longest we've ever gone except in summer vacations. I type: "sorry about last Wednesday."

"good."

"you dont sound like you mean it. i mean it. im really sorry."

No answer. I count the seconds. So many seconds. What a terrible, mean person I was to him. Vicious. I deserve for him to walk away and never come back.

He's not answering.

Don't walk away from me, Owen.

He's still not answering.

Please.

It's three whole minutes before his words show again.

"its ok. i was being a jerk."

I type fast: "no you weren't. i was. i was horrible. im sorry."

"i still love u. so whats up?"

I could cry from relief, but his words make me smile instead. Owen always goes straight to the point. He's so easy to understand. Such a good guy. "i have a calculus Q. how r exponential and logarithmic functions inverses of each other if they give the same graph?"

"One is in terms of what x equals. The other is in terms of what y equals. So theyre inverted ways of stating the same relationship."

God. How obvious. I type: "thnx."

"one more thing. the mind is a drunken monkey bitten by a scorpion."

I type: "r u completely fried?"

"i read it. the point of yoga is to still the mind . . . the crazy monkey. if you find that quiet place you wont get so angry."

I feel challenged. I type: "yoga has lots of points."

"no doubt. walk u home tomorrow?"

Tomorrow's Wednesday. Jazz Dance Club. I type: "k"

The rest of the math homework goes fast. Good. Time is passing. I've got to rush. I have somewhere to be.

I open Ovid to the story about Philomena. And, oh my God, this is not a happy tale. Hideous acts lead to unbelievably hideous acts, until a mother kills her son and bakes him in a pie she feeds to her husband. It's worse than a pony dying from rain. Ovid is demented to have made that tale into poetry. And Mrs. Reynolds is demented to have assigned it.

I search around for my biology text. It always makes sense. But I glance at the clock for the nine hundredth time. It's almost eleven. The evening is gone. My arms go weak, my legs and back, weak. I let myself drop softly to my knees.

I have managed to keep my mind off what's coming next purely by racing at full speed, swift that I am, tuna that I am. Which is appropriate, because this is a race. Vitiligo waits for no man. Or woman. Forget biology. Time's up.

It's Tuesday night. Exactly two weeks since I woke up with white lips. Two weeks—I can't believe so much has happened between Joshua and me in only two weeks. We're on fast forward.

But really it hasn't felt fast. It's felt like an eternity. As though Joshua and I have really been on this track since we were kids, we just didn't know it. And once we realized that, we picked up where we'd left off. It's been almost slow motion, looked at that way. Slow and inevitable. Tonight's inevitable, too. Or I hope it will be.

I creep downstairs and out of the house, and run flat out to the gazebo in the Weisskopfs' backyard, next door.

"Joshua?" I whisper loudly. It's very dark. Clouds cover the moon and the stars. Perfect.

"Here I am." He steps off the edge of the gazebo and hugs me.

I'm so glad to be in his arms. I lift my face to his and we kiss. "You smell like cinnamon."

"Sweet potato pie."

"Don't tell me you cooked your arch."

"New sweet potatoes. Mrs. Spinelli actually liked the idea of building models out of sweet potatoes. No harm to the environment and all that. Turns out she hates Styrofoam. So she said she'd give extra credit from now on to anyone who does projects with biodegradable materials. And she brought in a recipe this morning for sweet potato pie and told us all to try it, so we can see how great the aftermath of a sweet-potato project could be. She's, I don't know..."

"Eccentric?"

"I was going to say whack."

"And you tried the recipe?"

"My mother did."

"You asked her to?"

"Well, yeah. I couldn't help it. Mrs. Spinelli named the recipe Joshua's Sweet P Pie—I mean, what could I do?"

I don't really care about recipes right now. My hands are shaking. It's time time time. I kiss Joshua hard. My hands slide up into his curly hair and hold his head fast.

He makes a contented, muffly sound. "What's so urgent that it couldn't wait for lunch tomorrow?"

"Aren't you glad to see me?"

"Of course I am. I'm just kind of behind in physics. But I'd rather be with you any day. What's up?"

I loop my fingers over his belt and pull him into the gazebo.

"Good start," he breathes.

I undo his belt.

His hands are on my upper arms. He's breathing so deeply I can feel his belly move in and out against my hand. "Do you know what you're doing?"

"You can tell me if I do it wrong."

He gives a small laugh. "That isn't what I meant." His lips make a little noise, like he just gulped. "Have you thought about this?"

Have I thought about anything else? I unzip him.

"We, uh, we're going pretty fast, Sep. It's only been a little while since we started talking to each other again."

"It's been weeks."

"Two. Two weeks. I've kept track. That's not much, Sep. What's the rush?"

"Do you want us to stop?"

"No. That's not what I mean."

"Are you sure?" I ask.

"I'm sure. But are you? Are you sure, Sep?"

I pull down his trousers.

He makes that gulping noise again. "Good answer." His voice is husky.

I push him lightly so he drops onto the curving bench on this side of the round table. I get on my knees and push his legs further apart and insert myself between them and fondle him through the cloth. He breathes so hard, I sense his whole torso rise and fall. I pull down on his boxers and he lifts his butt just enough so that I can get them down past his knees.

He lets out a half grunt.

"Did I hurt you?"

"No. It's good." He reaches down to a pocket and pulls out something.

I'm clumsy. I have to try to go slow—careful. But all I can think about is how hard he is. And how silky soft the skin on the tip is. I brush my cheek against it.

He makes a noise as though he's having trouble catching his breath. I love that I can do that to him.

I can't stop. I can't think. It's like my whole body has become my cheeks and lips and tongue.

Almost instantly, he clamps a handkerchief over himself and groans. He jams the handkerchief back in his pocket, and stands, drawing me up with him. He pulls up his boxers and trousers, and buckles his belt. And I'm still panting, still inside that other place, that other feeling. He kisses me. "I didn't expect that." His voice is so quiet I can hardly hear it.

"Mmm," I manage. I try to slow my heart. "I could tell. Do you always have a handkerchief in your pocket?"

"Actually, yes. You never know when it will come in handy." He laughs.

"I don't get it."

"Masturbation."

"Oh. Yeah. I'm just not quite, you know, thinking straight yet."

"You're amazing," he says.

"I'm glad you liked it."

"I loved it. Your turn now."

"What?"

"Your sex manual didn't explain turn taking?"

"I don't have a sex manual."

"Then that truly was amazing. You're a natural. So relax now, and let me take over. Let it happen naturally." He unsnaps my jeans and opens the zipper and pulls my pants all the way off, yanking them over my sneakers.

And now I'm glad it's too dark to see.

It's a warm enough night, but still I get goose bumps. "I don't take anything. You know, like birth control pills."

"What we're going to do can't make you pregnant."

Well, of course not. He has his jeans on. What a dumb thing I said.

He pulls off my panties.

I'm standing with the bottom half of me naked in my neighbors' gazebo. Or naked except for my shoes and socks.

He kneels in front of me and runs his hands up and down my legs. They go over that ghost of a spot on the inside of my right thigh. The newest spot, and the biggest one yet. It's still faint, barely there, so it might not even be a spot—it might just be my fears. But so far all my fears have come true. His hands touch it and keep moving. His eyes don't see. Thank you, clouds. Thank you, thank you.

His hands go everywhere, till I'm wobbling so bad I think I'll fall.

He pulls me down beside him on the floor of the gazebo and stretches out on his back. "Straddle my face."

"What?"

"Just do it. One knee on either side of my head. Just do it."

"Facing which way?"

He laughs. "Facing the top of my head."

I straddle him and he pushes my knees out, till I'm low enough. He kisses the inside of one thigh, then the other. So soft it's like the best dream. Then his tongue flicks. Zap, like an electric shock. I jerk upward, rigid and more alive than I've ever been. He pulls me down again and holds me tight. And I implode, I explode, I fly apart, my head is twirling and I'm moving so fast, on and on and on, till it finally ebbs. And ends.

I clap my hand over his mouth to make him stop, and I collapse beside him.

He kisses my hand. Then my lips. "You're a wonder."

"I had an orgasm," I say between pants. "I came. I really came."

"Yeah." He laughs. "I could tell."

I like the way he does that. The way he takes words and turns them back on me. It's just a little thing, but right now it seems huge, earth-shattering. "I never came before."

"I wouldn't have known it."

"If that had lasted one more second, I think I would have vaporized."

"That's what it sounded like. I was afraid you'd wake the whole neighborhood."

I'm surprised and a bit chagrined. "Was I noisy?"

He laughs again. "Didn't you know? Yes. Yes, Sep, you were noisy. Very noisy."

"Oh."

"I loved it. And I love the little purring noises you make when we kiss."

"Do I make purring noises when we kiss?"

"Yes."

"You groaned. And I loved that, too."

"Well, good, 'cause you're stuck with me now." His teeth gleam white in that terrific smile of his.

And suddenly I realize I can see him! Oh no, the lights are on in the Weisskopfs' house. Someone's coming out the back door with a flashlight. Mr. Weisskopf! I stand and the light centers on my crotch.

I put my hands over my face. "Run," I say. "Run home."

I grab my jeans and feel around for my panties and give up and dash straight for my back door.

I lock it behind me and pull on my jeans. Then I tiptoe up the stairs as fast as I can and jump in bed.

I'm such an idiot. I should have run down the block and come back later, after Mr. Weisskopf went back inside. Now he knows it was me.

And he has my panties, to prove it.

Only how could I run down the block with no bottoms on?

I wait for the doorbell to ring. Or the phone.

I imagine Mamma's face when she gets the news. And Dad's. And Dante's.

I stare through the dark at the ceiling.

Nothing happens.

I think of bewildered Mr. Weisskopf, his flashlight illuminating the triangle of my pubic hair in his backyard gazebo. I pull the pillow over my mouth and laugh.

I did it. Even though I doubt Ms. Martin meant anything like this when she encouraged me to be a warrior, I feel the triumph of a warrior. It doesn't matter that I started off awkward, I stood up for myself. I was brave.

And I made Joshua happy.

Vitiligo hasn't stopped me. Yet.

26

A SMALL PAPER BAG drops on the table in front of me. It's crumpled. I look up.

Joshua's smiling. "Any repercussions?"

"Not yet."

"Maybe there won't be. Look in the bag."

I reach my hand in.

"No!" Joshua leans over. "Don't take it out. Just look inside."

And there are my panties.

"Thanks." I smile up at him. "But repercussions will follow. Mr. Weisskopf must have seen me go in my back door."

"Maybe not. I ran around a tree a couple of times, dangling your panties in my hand like a flag. I think he was so confused by that, he kept his eyes on me."

"Really?"

"Really."

I laugh.

Joshua laughs, too, and he's shaking his head. "He flashed that light and you covered your face instead of your crotch."

"In my neighborhood we don't recognize each other by our crotches, Joshua."

He laughs harder. "I can still see the whole scene."

"Sit down, you big goof. People are looking at us."

He sobers up. "I can't. The team's having lunch together again. Most of us, anyway. Coach might actually cancel practice because the rain's so hard. I'll talk to you tonight?"

I nod.

He pulls a plastic container out of his pack and a little plastic fork and sets it on the table.

"What's this?"

"I saved you some. But I wasn't real careful, so maybe it got jumbled up. Still, it should taste good. The recipe's in the bag with the panties." He takes a step backward and turns, and I miss him already. But then he spins on his heel and comes back and stands in front of me again. He taps his temple and he's grinning like a madman, like he's so full of whatever it is he has to say that he's about to burst.

I grin back. "What?"

"You're in my head. Always."

And he's gone.

I open the plastic container. There's a mashed piece of sweet potato pie. Joshua's Sweet-P Pie. I eat it slowly, even though I haven't yet touched my sandwich.

There is something corny about Joshua Winer. Corny and wonderful. It makes me feel corny. Like I'll blurt out that I love him or something.

A spasm of cold fear shoots up my spine.

I have a boyfriend. I used to tell myself I was in no hurry for romance. There was plenty of time for that later, when I was older. Then vitiligo changed the clock on me. And here I am. And it's all so unutterably dangerous, this romance thing.

But so is crossing the street. If there's a drunk driver around.

And so is eating produce in a restaurant. If they haven't cleaned it properly.

The memory of a little boy named James hits me like a granite slab. When I was in nursery school, James fell off the swing and broke his neck. Died—from such an every-day thing—swinging on a playground swing.

Life is dangerous.

But we have to live it. Right? Sex, like crossing the street, like swinging, is part of living. We have to take our chances.

The only question is when.

And, oh my God, my body sure is telling me that when is now.

Sex doesn't seem dangerous around Joshua.

Love does.

That's why I'm shivering now.

What if I love Joshua and then he walks away? He could. Boys have eyes. Every time Joshua says I'm beautiful, he reminds me of that.

I jam the bag of panties into my pocket and put the plastic container and fork in my lunch bag. Forget my sandwich. I'm off to the library.

And there they all are, nine hundred articles about love.

How do lovers act? Do they stick together or not?

I skip around various sites for a long time. If love can be measured in terms of lifelong pairings, the Kingdom Animalia is stingy on love.

The whole Phylum Arthropoda, insects and crawly stuff, seems crazy. I mean, look at praying mantises. The male mates for up to six hours (oh my God), then flies away unless the female bites off his head first. I doubt male mantises have any idea of the chance they're taking, but if they do, that's as close to devotion as insects get.

This is significant. There are zillions of insects. If you had a giant balance scale and put all the insects on one side and all the vertebrates and mollusks on the other, the insects would outweigh them. Even including elephants and whales.

So you might figure that what insects do is the general rule for animals. And since there is no love outside the Kingdom Animalia (you don't see affection in trees or sponges), you could say generalizations about insects show how the world works.

On the other hand, people aren't insects.

What really matters, at least to me, is what members of the Phylum Chordata, the vertebrates, do. Humans' phylum. Joshua's phylum.

Like fish. The male anglerfish attaches onto a female and his body grows together with hers. He withers and becomes nothing but a source of sperm. I could do without that kind of devotion. I want a whole lot more from Joshua than just sperm.

Seahorses—some choose a mate for life. Some are serially monogamous—with a different mate each breeding season. And some take mates any old time, blithely.

Birds seem haphazard. Flamingoes mate for life, ducks for a season, and most others have lots of trysts. Even those who take a mate for a season fool around, so that clutches contain eggs fertilized by several males.

Mammals seem random, too. Any male hamster will jump on any female hamster. But gerbils, their genetic cousins, form pairs or triads for life.

And, oh my God, bonobos, their promiscuity is amazing—they're gleefully sexual with everyone—males with males, and females with females, and males with females—a great big orgy.

Maybe only three percent of mammals mate for life. And humans aren't among them. I rub my hands to warm them up, but it doesn't help because I'm feeling cold all over.

I have to think straight. Mating for life isn't the same as loving. It can't be, or humans wouldn't have any idea of what love is. But we do. Just look at poetry, novels, movies, plays, songs.

Hey, so many of them are about unrequited love. Or breakups.

So maybe I have found what I was looking for, after all—the big answer. Chances are, if I fall in love with Joshua, he will leave me. That's what happens.

And it'll happen regardless of vitiligo. Even if he never finds out, he'll leave me. Joshua Winer will walk out of my life sooner or later. And given that we're only sixteen, probably sooner.

So do I let myself love him or not? If I have any control over it, that is.

The question: Is it better to have loved and lost than never to have loved at all?

I think of Joshua's finger tapping his temple. His words: "You're in my head. Always."

Then I laugh. The answer is so obvious.

Yes, Mr. Tennyson. Damn straight it's better to have loved and lost than never to have loved at all.

IT'S A TOE DAY. Ms. Martin is talking about connections between our toes and our arches. She says when we make those connections, we'll have intelligent feet. And this morning Mr. Dupris told us that flamingoes walk on their tiptoes. He sang "Tiptoe Through the Tulips." Everyone groaned, but he wasn't half-bad. Anyway, it's true. What we think are flamingoes' knees, bending backward, are really ankles. Their knees are hidden under their feathers. And what we think are their feet are really their toes. It turns out tons of animals go on tiptoe. Even elephants.

Now I mimic Ms. Martin in stance. I imagine that a

giant hook from the sky is connected by a filament to the center of the top of my skull, and the rest of me falls downward, weighted equally around my long, straight spine. I am one tall *Homo sapiens* on intelligent feet.

"Sit now. Sit in Baddha Konasana."

We all drop to sitting and look around to see who remembers what pose that is.

"Bottoms of your feet together. Sit tall, with your hands holding your feet and let your knees open to the sides in an act of compassion."

Someone whispers, "What guy paid her to say that?"

People giggle. But I'm listening closely.

"On an exhalation, relax your eyes and let gratitude allow your top eyelid to meet your bottom lid."

Compassion and gratitude. Who am I showing compassion to when I open my knees? Someone else, or myself?

Owen said the point of yoga is to still the drunken poisoned monkey inside us. Maybe he's right; maybe the monkey is easing up a bit. I feel almost calm. I'm focusing on the present. Specifically, on this pose. That was Mamma's advice. That's what Ms. Martin always says. The present.

I can sense a change in the room, but I don't know what it is.

As if by some secret cue, Melanie and Becca stand up and go to the closet where the CD player is. Everyone opens their eyes at the noise and drops into a more relaxed position, which I find strange, since nothing could be more natural for the body than the pose we were already in.

We all get to our feet and Ms. Martin retreats to a chair at the side of the gym.

The music comes on and Becca's at the front and we all just do what she does. It's a singer today, with a honeyed voice. I bet the name of the song is "Afro Blue" because that's in the refrain. It's sad and sexy at the same time.

Becca teaches us a routine. I love learning routines. Once you finally get them and you don't have to scramble to remember what comes next, you can put your energy into finding out how far you can go with each move. You can make the routine yours. Your body takes over. You dance.

I pound the routine into my head.

Then I surrender to my body. And my body does what it should. My arms transfer energy one to the other as though they're connected through the center of me. I twist my spine so far, I can feel my kidneys sing. Whoosh, and my torso swings down between my straight V legs and I'm looking at the rear wall and reaching for it. This is good. Something is going right. Whatever war my skin is waging against me, my muscles don't have any part in it. This is good. Really good.

Sweat-drenched, we stagger off to the locker room. I

hold back and wait for the others to shower first. Some of the senior girls strip completely before they step inside the shower curtain. Most girls strip down only to their panties and bra, though, then go inside the shower curtain and hang their undies over the curtain while they wash. No one goes inside the shower curtain fully dressed.

But that's what I'm going to do. And I figure it's less likely anyone will notice if I wait till everyone else has had their turn.

I'm wearing tights under my shorts and a shirt that goes down over my elbows. It's still too warm out for tights, but the splotch on the inside of my thigh is low enough that it showed when I tried on my shorts this morning. So I threw tights into my backpack along with the shorts.

I sit on the bench and look down at my feet, so I won't be tempted to look in the mirror and search for hints of new spots. Mirror checking threatens to become an obsession.

"You didn't do so bad today, girls," says Becca, buttoning up her shirt and addressing all of us as a group. She was the first to finish showering—the queen. She doesn't mean to act superior, I know. She's just trying to be encouraging. But she comes off as self-satisfied.

As if she heard my thoughts, Becca jerks her chin toward me. "You like Oscar Brown, Junior, huh, Sep?"

So that's the name of the jazz singer today. I give a small smile. Then I get up and stick my head in my locker and pretend to be looking for something.

"You were really into it out there." Her voice is friendly. "I bet Joshua would have liked to see that. You're becoming a sexpot. Even the way you walk down the halls, it shows."

I push my head so far into the locker now, it presses against the back wall.

"Well, see you all next week." I hear Becca's locker door slam.

I wait a while, then I straighten up, open my math book, and stand in front of my open locker, reading.

The conversation dribbles away to nothing.

"You can shower now, Sep." It's Melanie. She's come over behind me.

The way she says it discourages me. I'm going to wind up getting a reputation as a weirdo about shower behavior even before everyone sees my vitiligo and finds out how truly weird I am.

I close my locker and go over to a shower stall and step inside the curtain, then I strip and turn the water on to the hottest it will go. Steam comes up. School sets the water heater higher than we set it at home. I love the school shower.

I stand a long time with the water beating on my neck and back and butt.

Then I remember Owen. I agreed to walk home with him today. He's waiting for me.

Quick, I slip on my panties and bra and peek around the curtain.

Melanie's sitting on the bench looking at me. "You modest?"

I retreat behind the curtain and put on my shirt. It covers the spots on my belly and back and on my upper arm and elbow. But there's no point in putting on my tights and shorts, because I want to change into my jeans to go home. I hold my tights and shorts in front of my thighs. Okay, this works. No white spots show now, though the one on the back of my hand almost shows; the three red magic marker dots have washed to light pink.

I come out.

Melanie glances up from tying her sandals. They're the classic kind that lace halfway up your calf. "You did look good again today. Becca wasn't exaggerating."

"Thanks." I look at the tattoo on her ankle and wonder about what Joshua said. "You're here kind of late."

"I was waiting for a call from my little brother. He was supposed to tell me where to meet him. It's our dad's birthday tonight and we have a plan. But Raymond flaked out on me. Like usual. He didn't answer my texts—he didn't answer my calls—and now he just texted me and said we'll do it tomorrow, as though birthdays can be pushed around however you want. He can be such a jerk."

"I get it." I smile. "I've got a little brother, too."

"Oh, yeah? Well, I'm off. Want to walk home together?"

I blink. Am I imagining things or is there something wistful in the way she says it? "I'm already walking home with someone."

"Joshua?"

"No." But that feels too abrupt. After all, Becca mentioned Joshua, so it isn't like Melanie's being nosy. "Owen."

"He's nice." She rubs the top of her thighs and stands. "Well, another time."

I walk to my locker and open the door to hide behind it. Melanie's footsteps retreat and I hear the door open and close. I pull on my jeans and stuff my shorts and tights in my pack and run for the parking lot.

Owen's standing at the edge of the lot, near the activity bus stop. "So you didn't forget about me?"

"Sorry. I got involved with a shower."

He nods. "I thought only guys did that."

"Owen! I'm shocked." I slap my hands on my chest dramatically. "What's gotten into you?"

"How are you liking logarithms?"

"You're changing the subject. And not artfully. I already had logarithms in trigonometry last year. I just forgot. Sorry I sent you that stupid text last night—every year I seem to have to start at the beginning all over again. It's discouraging."

"I'm the same way."

We cross the street and I realize I'm a ball of tension. I let my arms give a quick shake to release the muscles. "No you're not, Owen. But I won't stand in the way of your being nice if you want."

"I'm not being nice. It's true. Math is like that. You have to learn things a dozen times before they sink in enough to be part of you."

I wonder if that's so. In elementary and middle school the math lessons at the beginning of the year were always review. I resented them. But maybe they weren't a waste of time after all.

I look around. Melanie must have taken a different route. But what a stupid thought—I don't even know where she lives.

"Looking for someone?"

I shouldn't be. I'm not even really friends with Melanie. "What do you know about tattoos, Owen?"

"You thinking of getting one?"

"No. I thought about it, but decided it wouldn't serve my purposes, after all."

"'Wouldn't serve your purposes,' huh? You sound mysterious."

"I'm not."

"So if you're not going to get one, why are you talking about them?"

"I just want to know what you know about them."

"Less than you do. But I do know people often regret them. This counselor at camp when I was just a kid—"

"You mean last year?"

"You want to hear or you want to make fun of me?"

"Sorry. Tell me."

"She said that her cousin got a tattoo when she was eighteen, of her favorite movie star."

"That doesn't sound bad."

"Exactly. That's the point. To teenage girls it doesn't sound bad. And if she had gotten it ten years before, she'd have chosen a spotted dog or a pink dinosaur or something. So how do you think she felt about that movie star ten years later?"

I laugh. "Good point." I rip a leaf off a bush as we pass. "Ever heard that some tattoos have meaning? I mean, of course they have meaning, but, you know, that some send a kind of message?"

"You're either being obscure or you're an idiot, Sep. Tattoos can mean all sorts of things."

"What about pink triangles?"

"On the ankle? For lesbians?"

So Owen knows, too. I can't believe it. "How long have you known that, Owen?"

"About those triangles? Since last year. Why?"

"How did you find out?"

"What are you talking about, Sep? They were a big deal. Everyone knew."

"I didn't. What if I had gotten a pink triangle on my ankle just by accident?"

"Well, you'd have been screwed."

"So screwed."

"Yeah."

"Major screwed."

"Yeah."

"And all by accident. Do you ever think about how many things happen to us just by accident, Owen?"

"Of course. But I don't dwell on it, Sep. You can't do anything about accidents."

We walk a couple of blocks in silence and cut through the woodsy area by the condominiums. Owen slips off his backpack as he walks, reaches in, and hands me a book. Then he puts his backpack on again.

I look at the title. *The Things They Carried*. "What's this?"

"A gift. I put it in my pack yesterday, after you

apologized. It's appropriate, because you cussed last time we were together."

"Is it about cussing?"

"And other things. The Vietnam War."

"You care about the Vietnam War?"

"If you read it, you will, too. Ordinary people, just a little older than us, wound up halfway around the world shooting at people and getting shot at and trying to figure out what it means."

"What war means?"

"War. Life. Everything." Owen's voice goes suddenly thick with emotion. He hardly ever gets emotional. His dad has diabetes, the bad kind that you get when you're little, and I was with him once when his dad went into diabetic shock, so I know: Owen is a rock. Or at least he tries to be.

I move closer. "They had the draft then," I say softly. "Nonno talked about it once, about what a lousy system it was. Italy was different. In Italy every guy did military service after high school, no matter what."

"That had to suck."

"Yeah. But it was fair. Nonno was big on being fair."

"Does anyone sit in his chair yet?"

"Just Rattle."

"Time," says Owen. He clears his throat. "Some things take time."

"I guess. At least we don't have the draft anymore. We won't wind up in the middle of a war like the characters in this book."

"We have to figure out what it all means anyway, Sep, no matter where we are." He hooks his thumbs through his backpack straps and hikes the pack up his back a little. "Besides, we sort of are in the middle of a war. All of us. The same big war. 'Cause all these wars, they're all connected."

"You're lecturing me now."

"Sorry." He shrugs. "I'm bad at apologies. Here I go offending you when the book's supposed to be an apology."

"For what?"

"For last time. I understand you feel lousy, even if you don't want to tell me about it. You've got things to figure out—like we were saying. I'm sorry I tried to minimize it. I was stupid enough to think that might help."

I feel off-balance. I'm the one who was in the wrong— but Owen actually understands why I acted so bad. I want to thank him profusely. But I know if I try, I'll get all sappy. And something's already too sad in this conversation. Without a word, I slip off my backpack, slide in the book, and sling the pack back on.

"So how's it going, Sep?"

"I can't complain." Which isn't true. I complain all the

time. But Owen's just getting the conversation going again. The least I can do is try to be cooperative. "What about you? Spending a lot of time at that website? The one of the political genius?"

"Chomsky dot info. Have you looked at it?"

"No."

"You're making a mistake."

"I'll look. I've had other things on my mind."

"You and Joshua—how's that working out for you?"

There's something in his voice that makes it seem like a challenge. "Why do you want to know?"

"Uh, let's see. We've been friends for years and something new and major happens in your life. Could that be it?"

"We're getting along good."

"That's great."

We come out on the other side of the condos and turn up Milton Street.

"But we won't be together for long."

"What do you mean?" says Owen.

"Things happen. Accidents. Like you said, you can't do anything about accidents."

"Could you be a bit more edifying?"

"No."

"Am I supposed to guess?"

"I don't want to talk about it."

"You brought it up."

"So I'm burying it."

"Well, I'm still above ground. Remember that later."

"What's that mean, Owen?"

"You're smart; figure it out." The corner of his mouth twitches, as though he's fighting to control himself. He turns at his street without a farewell. His shoulders are squared, like he's marching away.

I stare after him. Owen. He's the first one I bounce ideas off, especially school stuff that Devin would hate talking about. He's always there. We're good friends. But this year is different. And he just gave me a gift—a used book, but a gift anyway. I swallow. In that text message when I apologized for being such a jerk, he wrote, "I still love you." I say it to him all the time, but he never says it back. Only he did in that message. Oh my God, anyone else in the world would have figured it out long ago: Owen likes me. That way. And all along I thought I understood him—I thought he was so easy to understand.

An enormous sadness weighs me down.

I touch my lips. They're cinnamon red today. Devin gave me a new lipstick out of the blue on Sunday, when I borrowed the sex novels. She's wearing lipstick to school these days, too. Solidarity.

I put on lipstick the first day of school and Joshua came

after me full throttle. Oh, I responded all right. But he initiated it. And lipstick just might have been the ignition.

But then Melanie—it felt like she was flirting with me—or almost—'cause why would she offer to walk home together when she doesn't even know if I live near her—unless she does know, which means she had to find out.

And now Owen.

And I don't think lipstick is what's making Melanie or Owen notice me.

It's like being with Joshua has changed me. Maybe I'm giving off a signal that says "come hither." Pheromones, like a moth or a hamster. I'm even walking different—that's what Becca said in the locker room. Is that what sex does to you, make other people perceive you differently?

Well, I don't want this. I want Joshua. I want whatever can happen with Joshua before my world turns to slime. But I don't want anyone else's attentions. I don't want to hurt anyone's feelings. Not Melanie's. And not Owen's. Never, never Owen's.

28

I'M READING POETRY BY Langston Hughes. Oh, poet, where have you been all my life? We've got ten poems in our school textbook, but Mr. Batell told us to hit the library and find more and memorize our favorite one, because he's going to call on some of us at random to recite. Which means, of course, that we all hit the Internet instead, and we'll probably all come in with the same poem tomorrow. But that's okay. I can stand to hear any one of Langston Hughes's poems twenty times, a hundred times, nine hundred times.

And some of us actually made it into the library. I did.

Langston Hughes wrote novels and short stories and plays, too. But I don't want to read them. I mean, they might be as fantastic as his poetry, but it would kill me if they were. His poetry is diamond hard. The only thing that keeps me from bleeding out entirely is the brevity.

So maybe I couldn't survive hearing one of his poems nine hundred times, after all.

I started out by reading his collection *Ask Your Mama: 12 Moods for Jazz*. I chose it because I'm the only one of my friends who calls her mother Mamma, though Langston Hughes spells it with one M.

That Hughes collection is okay. More than okay. And jazz influenced this poet, that's for sure. You hear it in the rhythms. An improvisational air. But other poems of his do more for me. Like "Dream Deferred"—that poem turns me inside-out. It dares you to be honest.

Honest.

What I honestly want is to enjoy what Joshua and I have together while I can. I haven't hurt anyone.

But I might. If I keep this up.

That's the honest truth.

I put my notebook back in my bottom drawer and walk through the house searching for Mamma. She's in her study, taking laundry out of the dryer. Mamma doesn't like us to use the dryer. She says things like, "What's the sun for?" and makes us all hang the laundry out.

Today, though, it rained hard, and even when it stopped, the air hung wet everywhere. So Mamma relented.

"Is it really your week to do the laundry?" I frown. "I thought it was mine."

"It probably is. Come help me."

"Later. After we get back from the mall."

Mamma sticks her tongue in her cheek and I can tell she's chewing on it. "We're going to the mall?"

"Please?"

"It's Wednesday. I thought that was a Thursday routine. After seeing Dr. Ratner."

"We're not going back to Dr. Ratner till the middle of next month, remember? I can't wait that long."

She shakes out one of Dante's T-shirts and smooths it on her belly, then folds slowly. "Mr. Weisskopf caught a couple of teens in his gazebo last night. Do you know anything about that?"

"Is that all he told you?"

"He thought the girl might have been you. But he didn't get a good look."

"Is that what he said? That he didn't get a good look?"

"Yes."

Mr. Weisskopf is more discreet than I'd have guessed. "I've got nothing to add."

"Hmmm. I'm doing my best not to get angry here, Pina."

"The mall, Mamma."

"Don't change the subject."

"That is the subject. The mall. Can we go? I'll fold all the rest of this when we get back. Promise."

"How many lipsticks do you own now, Pina?"

"What do you care? I buy them with my babysitting money."

"I don't care about the money. I care about you."

"I'm not going to buy more lipstick."

"What are you going to buy?"

"Do I really deserve this third degree?"

"I don't know, Pina. Do you?"

"Okay, I'll walk to the mall."

"You're grounded, remember."

"You let me go to the mall last week."

"It's too late. You'll never make it back in time for dinner."

"Unless you drive me."

Mamma picks up another T-shirt and chews on her tongue. Then she throws the shirt back on the pile and slaps a hand on her forehead. It stays there a long moment. "Get the keys."

I knew it. Mamma has no experience at being a prison guard. I actually feel sorry for her right now.

Once at the mall I ditch Mamma at the drugstore and make a beeline for Slinky's cosmetics counter.

"Hey," she calls. "Come to show it off?"

"What?"

"The tattoo. Or is it tattoos?"

"I chickened out."

"Good for you. With a tattoo, you'd have never been able to get a job with the CIA."

"I never want a job with the CIA."

"It's just an example, kiddo. Imagine holding out your tattooed hand for a shake at a job interview. The interviewer would fumigate his office after you left. You dodged the bullet, sweetie. There are better ways to be cool."

"Don't be such a mother," I say with more force than I intended.

"Sorry. I just mean, if you need to express yourself, you could think of other ways. So what's up?"

"Are you married, Slinky?"

"Slinky?" She smiles and tilts her head. "Are you kidding? You know I have a boyfriend."

"I mean, were you?"

"What is it you really want to ask?"

"Well, you have a child and everything." I shrug one shoulder. "That must have been an accident?"

"A surprise. There's a difference. I get the feeling you're still not asking what you want."

"Slinky, I've been thinking of jumping my boyfriend."

"Oh, yeah?" Her face changes, but I can't read it. The smile is gone.

"I sort of already jumped him. But not completely, you know."

"I guess I do." She leans on the counter. "So . . . are you asking me whether it's worth the risk of pregnancy?" Her voice is very soft.

"I don't think I'm really asking anything. I just want someone to know."

"I've been there before. Listen up: telling me doesn't make me share the responsibility."

How she can cut straight to the quick like that astonishes me. I was right to come to her. "You're really a hard ass, Slinky."

"Is that why you're telling me? So I can be hard on you?"

"I don't want to hurt him."

"Who?"

"My boyfriend."

She pulls back and her eyebrows go up. "You think

you'll hurt him by sleeping with him? That's a new one. Isn't he in high school?"

"Yeah."

"You're telling me there exists a high school boy who's not dying to score?"

"I don't think this one is."

"Is he gay?"

"No way."

"Is he healthy?"

"He plays football."

"Oh, come on. This guy is dying to score."

"He's not the typical football player."

"What, you're buddies with the whole team? I wouldn't have pegged you for that."

"He's special."

"Sure. Everyone is. Let me tell you a secret." She leans even closer. "There's really only one question that's relevant to whether or not a high school football player wants to score."

"What's that?"

"Is he alive?"

I laugh, though I know it's not true.

But I let myself believe Slinky about Joshua—not in general, just with respect to me. I let myself believe it because I need to. Joshua wants to score with me, no matter what happens after that. Just like me, he's going to feel that it's better to have loved and lost than never to have loved at all—yup, that's exactly what he'll feel.

This is the belief I can run with.

29

THE FOOTBALL GAME THIS week was Friday again. I stayed home, still grounded, and finished all my homework for the weekend. But I took this babysitting gig on Saturday.

Here I am, holding an umbrella in one hand and ringing the Harrisons' doorbell with the other, looking like an ordinary honest person, like the person I used to be. Joshua will be coming over within a half hour. Mamma didn't ask, and I didn't tell.

"Hi, Pina." Mrs. Harrison opens the door and steps back. Mr. Harrison stands beside her and blinks. I wonder if he's confused that she just called me Pina when he seems to know I call myself Sep. "There's a plate of treats in the refrigerator. For you and Joshua."

My cheeks burn. If I'm this transparent to Mrs. Harrison, Mamma definitely knows. Well, fine. I hate being queen of deception. "That's very nice of you. Thanks." Oops. "I guess I owe you a bag of sweet potatoes." I laugh in embarrassment.

"No, no, it was nothing. Sarah told us about the wonderful arch. Have fun now." They leave. Without even kissing Sarah.

They must have kissed her before I rang the bell. They must have been standing at the door waiting for the bell to ring, like horses at the gate before a race, raring to go. It's later than they usually go out, but still, I'm surprised.

And it dawns on me: They're glad I've got a boyfriend. My first boyfriend. As long as I want a place to be alone with Joshua, they've got a sitter.

Symbiosis.

But their eagerness gives them away: they're worried it won't last. A teenage romance, after all. They'll take me while they can get me.

I hang my raincoat on the coatrack. I set the umbrella open beside it on the tiled entranceway. I nestle my rain boots in front of it.

Sarah's sitting on the living room floor. She still hasn't

acknowledged my presence. I walk over and plop down beside her. Legos again.

"The bottoms of your jeans are wet," says Sarah.

"It's raining."

"Like God crying," says Sarah.

"Where did you get that idea?"

"Clancy."

I remember the name vaguely. Oh, yes. "He's the one you bit?"

"He bit me, too."

"He said rain is God's tears?"

"He said rain is God's pee."

"What a nasty idea."

"I punched him. And I told him rain is God's tears."

"Rain is water from the clouds, Sarah."

"Clouds of God's tears."

I clear my throat. "Water on the earth—puddles and lakes and rivers and oceans, all that water—it sometimes gets absorbed into the air and forms clouds. And when the clouds get heavy enough, rain happens."

"God's unhappy," says Sarah.

Okay, another tack. "What would God have to be unhappy about?"

"Clancy."

I almost laugh. I guess if I were God, Clancy might make me inconsolable, too.

"When's Joshua coming?"

"Soon."

Sarah smiles to herself as she snaps a Lego wheel into place. "I have something for him."

A tiny sting of jealousy makes me sit up straight. "What?"

"You wouldn't like it."

I furrow my brows in suspicion. "What is it, Sarah?"

"You'll tell Mommy."

"Not unless she really should know."

She smirks.

The doorbell rings.

"Yay!" Sarah runs and lets Joshua in.

He drips on the entranceway floor and smiles at me.

"Don't you know about raincoats?" I say, not budging from my floor spot.

"My jacket's usually enough."

"Not tonight," I say.

"Not tonight." Joshua spies the coatrack. He peels off the wet jacket and hangs it near my raincoat.

"Your pants are wet," says Sarah.

"It's okay, Boss."

Sarah puts her hands on her hips.

"I mean, Sport."

She juts one hip out and mock pouts.

"I mean, Sarah."

Sarah laughs. "Come see." She grabs for his arm.

Joshua puts his hands up. "Whoa. Let me take these off first." He puts his wet sneakers beside my boots. Then he lets Sarah pull him past me and down the hall toward her bedroom.

"You stay there," she calls back to me.

I follow.

Sarah gets a flashlight from the nightstand beside her bed and opens her closet. She shines it in the corner.

Joshua gets on his knees and peers in.

I lean forward but it's impossible to see past his bulk.

"Sep, do you know where they keep the plastic bags?"

"Like a garbage bag?"

"He's not garbage." Sarah shakes Joshua's shoulder. "He's mine."

"A dead mouse does not belong to you," says Joshua.

"A dead mouse?" I squeak.

"Yes he does." Sarah pushes on Joshua's shoulder with both hands now. "I own him."

"No, you just discovered him."

"I found him in the yard. So he's mine."

"Did you carry him in?" I ask.

"Of course."

"With your hands?"

Sarah laughs at me. "I'm not a cat. I didn't carry him in my mouth."

"Mice are dirty, Sarah. Let's go wash your hands. And I'll get you a plastic bag, Joshua."

"Thief! I knew you wouldn't understand," Sarah says to me. "But you"—she turns to Joshua—"You should."

"What would you do with a mouse, anyway?" asks Joshua.

"Show him."

"What?"

"Show and tell. You know. Everyone does it."

"Your teacher wouldn't appreciate that," I say.

"Clancy would."

"Clancy? You and Clancy fight."

"Not about mice."

"Listen, Sarah, he's dirty. Never touch dead animals. You can pick up diseases."

"Meat is dead animals."

"But meat is refrigerated," I say.

"I'll put him in the refrigerator."

"No," I yelp.

Joshua wraps his arms around Sarah. He's still on his

knees and she's standing, so he's enveloping pretty much all of her. "This mouse is garbage, Sarah. You can't have him. If you want a live mouse, talk to your parents."

"Mommy hates live mice. So does Rucka."

Joshua closes Sarah tighter into his arms. He doesn't ask who Rucka is. I have to love him for that. "Tell you what. You can put the mouse in the plastic bag."

"No, she can't." I shake my head vigorously. "There are germs all over it."

"She already touched it, Sep. And she can scrub good afterward."

Sarah lifts her chin to me. Her eyes defy me to speak.

I get the plastic bag and watch Sarah lift a small, shriveled gray thing with pathetic little feet and claws, all curled and flimsy. She doesn't take it by the tail with just her thumb and index finger. She holds it in both hands, cradled, and slides it into the bag. For an instant, I'm sorry for her. And for the mouse.

I put the plastic bag on the kitchen counter and take Sarah to the bathroom. "Why not just bathe now? All over."

"Joshua has to stay out."

Joshua lifts his hands in surrender, like he did when Sarah grabbed for him at the front door. He backs out of the bathroom.

"That's okay," I say. "He can wait for us. He can choose a book for us to read afterward."

"Sure, I'll do that."

"Go!" orders Sarah. "Three."

"Three books, coming up." He heads for her bedroom.

Sarah bathes quickly. She can be no-nonsense when she wants. And around Joshua, she wants. "I'm done."

"Okay, stay a minute and let me go get your pj's." I go to her room.

Joshua's sitting on the bed reading *The Big Orange Splot*. He looks at me. "I love this book."

"I do, too. It's one of my favorites." My throat feels all lumpy, like I want to cry. "Do you know *Blue Moose*?"

He shakes his head.

"When's your birthday?"

"January."

I sort of remembered that. I snatch the pj's from under Sarah's pillow. "If I still know you then, I'll get it for you."

He grabs me by the wrist and pulls me onto his lap. "You better still know me then." He kisses me.

I get up all wobbly. How can it be that this boy has such an effect on me? I cannot wait to be with him.

I make it through drying and dressing Sarah. I make it through listening to Joshua read her *The Big Orange Splot*.

"What's next?" asks Sarah.

"I don't know," says Joshua.

"I told you to pick three," says Sarah.

"I thought you and Sep could each choose one."

"But I told you to pick all three."

"I got distracted. I love this one."

"You love it?"

"Yes," says Joshua.

"Really?"

"Yes."

"All right. You can read it two more times."

So Joshua reads *The Big Orange Splot* two more times. He does it with feeling. And Sarah listens, giving all her attention.

We both kiss her good night.

"Don't forget the snack," says Sarah.

"What?" asks Joshua.

"Mommy made it. I helped. Eat it."

We close her door and go down the hall.

Joshua's hand envelops mine.

"Do you want a snack?" I ask him.

"I want you."

"Good."

"But I have something for you first." He sits on the couch and pulls me down beside him. Then he digs in his pants pocket. "Here."

It's one of those rubber stamps that little kids use. This one is of a seahorse. "You thought about a tattoo, right? And you keep making designs on the back of your hand. Maybe you'd like to cover yourself in seahorses."

"Thank you."

"There's more." He digs in the other pocket and hands me a slim metal box.

I open it. It's an inkpad. Green. "Thank you." I set the stamp and inkpad on the coffee table. Then I grin at him. "Ready?"

He smiles and shakes his head. "You know what? I can't believe I'm saying this, but I think we ought to talk a little first."

I snuggle back beside him. "About what?"

"With you all close like this, my head empties." He laughs.

I put my hand over his heart. "Have you ever slept with anyone, Joshua?"

He gives a low whistle, leans forward with his forearms on his thighs, and folds his hands. He doesn't look at me. "Yes."

"Who was it? Sharon?"

"I can't tell. You know that. It would be telling you something personal about someone else, Sep."

"Was she on the pill?"

"I slept with two people. And one of them was on the pill. And I didn't ask the other one." He puts both hands in his hair and folds them around the back of his head and stares at the floor between his knees.

"You didn't ask?"

"She knew how to take care of herself."

"How can you be sure?"

"I am." He sighs and leans back and drops his hands to the sides of his thighs. "She'd had a lot of experience." He looks at me. "A lot."

"You've had a lot of experience."

"Me?"

"Two people, and you're only sixteen."

"Yeah. Yeah, compared to you, I've had a lot of experience."

"Weren't you afraid you'd get AIDS?"

"I was fourteen the first time. AIDS was the last thing on my mind."

"Fourteen." Ninth grade. Lord. "How old was she?"

"Come on, Sep. I won't identify her. She wanted to have fun. And she enjoyed teaching me things. And I enjoyed learning."

"You learned well."

"I'm glad you think so."

"I'm not on the pill, Joshua."

"I know. You told me Tuesday night. Remember? It doesn't have to be relevant, Sep. We can go slow."

"I don't want to go slow."

Our eyes lock.

"You're in a rush?" His voice trembles just the slightest bit.

"Yes."

"After the other night—you know, the gazebo—I kind of thought you might say that." He reaches into his pocket. "One more thing." He puts a foil wrapper on the coffee table.

It takes a few seconds for me to realize it's a condom.

I'm shaking all over. "Lights out," I whisper.

THE WEEKS GO BY in a bright blur, like a single wild sweep of a paintbrush across a white canvas, making colors dance everywhere. Joshua and I have lunch together every day. We text each other every night. We take walks on the weekend. And we make love.

You can call it having sex. But this pleasure is so much beyond anything I've read about in the nonhuman animal world, it's got to be making love.

Even for humans, this is no ordinary thing. I've prowled around the Internet, so I know. Whoever taught Joshua did a bang-up job. Or maybe he was just a gifted student.

When we're at the Harrisons', we do it on the floor now,

because it's too hard to manage the couch without falling off, given the way I throw myself around. I'm glad he uses a condom, because otherwise his sperm would get whiplash. And once we went back to the Weisskopfs' gazebo and did it. And once in the backseat of Mamma's old VW Beetle, which was actually a lot better than I thought it would be. Anyplace turns out to be fine, really.

Joshua is good to be with—every sense of *good*—deep down clean and pure good. He talks without hesitation, about anything. And I do the same. It's like we tumble together with abandon. We talk about things that have happened to us all through school. Big and little. We count on each other.

When Devin told me she'd been waiting her whole life to fall in love, and asked what I'd been waiting for, I didn't know. I really truly didn't. Now I do; now that I have it, this is it. I had no idea that people, ordinary people, could feel such joy.

The month of being grounded ended Monday. This weekend we have plans to go to our first party together. I am planning to dance with Joshua all night, dance crazy and wild, dance till I drop.

In Jazz Dance Club Ms. Martin beams at me. Melanie gives me a thumbs up. But even without them, I'd know it. This body is on a roll.

This is my happy blur. My blindingly colorful blur. It has nothing to do with white. I can almost forget white. I can almost forget vitiligo.

I am lucky. So very lucky.

That is the thought I have every morning, even as I pop my vitiligo vitamin pill.

And, oh dear God, this is the thought I have right now. At 6:30 a.m. on Wednesday morning. I am standing here looking in the mirror and then I see it.

The finger of white on my neck now juts past where a turtleneck can hide it. It splits and then splits again, like the tree-shape of a neuron. And, oh Lord, I see something else. My fingers reach up to my face toward the faint hint of a new spot going off from the top of the right side of my upper lip to my cheek, a hint that will assert itself if not tomorrow, then soon. Very soon. It's the size and shape of one of those ugly, fat, green worms that sometimes attack Mamma's tomato plants. My stomach turns.

Time has run out.

People battle time in a thousand ways. Women turning forty rush to get pregnant before they dry up forever. New parents take nine hundred photos of each stage of their baby's life before it's gone for eternity.

I rushed. And I made it in time. And now it's over. I press the heels of my hands against my eyes till the tears stop.

I've been lucky. I had more than a month with Joshua. Lucky.

Probably luckier than most girls. I bet first loves are full of insecurities about hair and teeth and breasts and pockets of fat, even the pitch of your voice and little speech habits you have and the way you talk too much and your stupid laugh and how you chew too loud and all that—all the things you're afraid someone else won't like. I didn't have that. Every time one of those anxieties dared to pop up, I just squelched it—I had no energy for it. It took all my effort just to hide my big secret . . . somehow I managed to shove it to some very deep and ancient part of my brain—maybe even to the brain stem, where it couldn't interfere with anything. My breathing, my heartbeat, my blood pressure, they all went on in spite of everything I was hiding. Joshua and me—we went on in spite of it. We were bigger than it. We were immune.

Except we weren't.

All that about tumbling together with abandon—what bullshit. I am the worst liar alive.

I tie a scarf around my neck and don't pack a lunch. I meet up with Devin and Becca and walk to school, silent, unable to even listen to them. I go to my first class. Then my second. Then the library. Joshua's waiting in the lunch-room, of course. I should tell him. But I don't want to risk crying at school. He'll assume something came up. He has a way of assuming the best.

I go to my third class, and fourth. I go to Jazz Dance Club. I take a shower.

Becca stands by her locker and asks, "What's up with the scarf?"

I realize now I wore it in the shower. I am a total flake. Now I'll have to go outside with a soaking scarf. I shake my head as Becca leaves.

"In the dumps?" asks Melanie.

I cannot look at her. If I meet anyone's eyes, I don't know if I'll be able to hold it in.

"Think pink," she says.

I don't even care what that means.

When I go outside there's Owen, reliable Owen, my Wednesday walk-home partner. Will Owen get labeled a freak when I am? Do I owe it to him to shoo him away?

Nah. It's no reflection on him that he walks home with me. No one will give him shit over it. Besides, if they do, or if he can't stand the sight of me, or whatever, he can simply stop.

We walk home and he tells me about some mathematical construct he's learned about called a lattice. In some other world, I think I might even care.

When I look at my cell after dinner, there's Joshua's message: "what's up? where were u 2day?"

I don't want to answer.

But I have to. I can't let him just wonder. The sooner he faces reality, the better.

There are nine hundred things I could say, ways I could ease into it. But what's the point? It's like when Nonna, my grandmother, was dying. Mamma spent a lot of time preparing us. But it hurt just the same as when Nonno simply dropped dead out of the blue. Gone is gone.

I type: "its over."

"whats over?"

I type: "u and me."

"what r u talking about?"

I turn off the cell and double over in pain. I've just plunged headfirst onto a sword. What must he be feeling?

I stretch out on the floor and take slow, deep breaths, but the huge ache won't stop.

I hold up the cell. Dead.

There are reasons why I did that. Right now, though, I can't think of a single one. I am the stupidest person in the world. No, I'm a nonperson. I'm not here, inside this body. I'm nowhere.

The kitchen phone rings. I yell out, "If it's for me, say

I died and moved to Minneapolis." Because if I talk to him now, I'll lose my resolve. Everything will spill out and then he'll be in the muck with me. Mired.

I do my homework and go to bed early. But I can't sleep. I toss all night. When the alarm rings, I want to throw the clock across the room. But I don't. I don't do anything. What's the use?

I look in the mirror. The spot on my face is still faint, like a whisper. The one on my neck is more distinct. And they're not spots—that's what Dr. Ratner calls them, but he's wrong. None of them are spots. They're blotches. Fat or skinny, they are horrible blotches.

I have one scarf in the world. So I tie it around my neck again.

Thursday is a repeat of Wednesday. I wonder if I'll lose weight, skipping lunch every day.

Joshua's waiting for me as I come out of my last class of the day. "What's going on?"

"I can't talk."

"Why not?"

I walk faster.

He steps in front of me. "Sep. Please. What happened?"

"I can't see you anymore." I look down at my shoes.

"Please look at me."

I won't cry here. I won't. He has to leave me alone. For

his own good—not just mine. But I owe him something; I force myself to look in his face.

His cheeks are flushed. His eyes glisten. "Did your parents find out? Because if they did . . ."

"No. It's not them."

"Then what? What happened?"

I press my lips together so hard they go numb.

"Did I do something? Tell me, Sep. I don't know what I did, and anyone has a right to that. Just tell me. Give me half a chance."

"You didn't do anything. No one did. You were wonderful, Joshua. You are wonderful. It just happened."

"What happened?"

"Something awful. Or I think it's going to get awful. And you shouldn't be part of it."

"I am part of it."

"No, you're not. And you won't want to be. Trust me. I have to face this alone."

"Whatever it is, I am part of it—because I'm with you."

I shake my head. "I have to go, Joshua."

"Are you pregnant?" he whispers.

"No!" He knows when I had my period and when we last slept together, so how can he ask that? I close my eyes and press the heels of my hands against my eyelids to stop the rush of tears. When I think I have it under control, I look at him again and murmur, "It isn't going to work. We're not going to work. And I really—really, really, really —can't talk about it."

His mouth drops open. His cheeks go slack. He looks like he'll cry, too. He lifts his hands out to both sides, then drops them. "I don't believe this." And his voice cracks midsentence.

"It's for your own good," I whisper.

"What does that mean?"

I turn and run.

Another evening of homework. And text messages I don't answer. Another night of twisting the sheets into knots.

Friday morning the tomato worm on my face is distinct. I stare in the mirror. It's so ugly, my stomach pitches. I retch into the toilet. I can't do this.

I go back to bed. I put a pillow over my face. Could a person hold a pillow down with enough force to smother herself or would she pass out before she could die?

"Hey, Slut, Ma says to get your ass down to the kitchen now."

I press the pillow harder.

Dante rips it off my face. He's staring down at me. "Holy shit."

"Yeah, holy shit, little brother."

"Ma's waiting."

"Tell her I died."

Dante walks to the door.

"Give me back my pillow."

He looks at me, then he leaves, with the pillow.

The idiot actually thought I might kill myself. That's how bad he thinks I look.

I stare at the green seahorse on the back of my hand. I stamped it there yesterday morning. It barely shows now. I could put green seahorses all over my face.

"Pina?" Mamma comes into the room. She sits on the bed beside me. She gathers my hands in hers.

"I'm not going to school today."

"All right."

"All right?" I sit up, rigid with instant fury. "Really? Are you going to let me stay in my room for the rest of my life?"

"You won't want to stay here for the rest of your life. But for today, yes. You can stay here."

"Don't be reasonable with me."

She hugs me.

I beat at her.

And she keeps hugging. Till we're both crying.

But it doesn't help.

The day is long and boring. I sleep on and off. I don't brush my teeth or comb my hair. Once I glance in the mirror and put both hands in my hair and thrash it around. I look like some lunatic in a B horror movie, the madwoman from the woods.

I read. I surf the Internet.

Mamma comes home at four. "Get your clothes on. We have an appointment with Dr. Ratner."

"You go."

She pulls the covers off me. "He was nice enough to fit us in at the end of his day. We're showing up."

"What am I supposed to do, put a bag over my head?"

"Just get your clothes on."

"Medicine can't do anything for me."

"That's right."

"So what's your point?"

"You'll see."

"I hate you," I yell.

She goes to my closet, takes out a pair of jeans, and tosses them on the foot of my bed. "We're going. Ten minutes."

31

THE CREAM IS NOT a bad match for my skin. Dr. Ratner is pretty observant. And so apologetic about how long it took for his order to arrive that I have to tell him it's all right to make him feel better. I rub it onto the back of my hand slowly. The color doesn't blend perfectly, but it's not bad.

He's writing in my chart, but I know he's checking me out with his peripheral vision. He's trying to be discreet. Like Mr. Weisskopf, saying he didn't get a good look at the teens in his gazebo.

All these adults who think they're so kind. They think

they know what it's like. But they don't. They can't even guess.

I can feel the fury ignite inside me again. Control it. Breathe deep. Count to nine hundred. Whatever it takes. Just don't keep yelling at people.

Except I haven't yelled at people. Only at Mamma. I look at her.

She's watching me.

"I'm sorry, Mamma."

She doesn't say anything.

Dr. Ratner looks inquisitively from me to Mamma and back to me.

"I yell at her," I say. "Please don't tell me not to. I already know I suck."

"Rage is a normal reaction, Sep." Dr. Ratner scratches his ear.

Does he realize he just used the N-word with me: *normal*? Is he about to apologize?

Dr. Ratner looks at me and raises his brows. "Well, what do you think of that cream?"

"Little old normal me will use it."

He blinks at my tone, and now I've hurt him, too. I really do suck.

"It's simply cosmetic," he says. "It won't change anything. But this brand doesn't come off that easily, so you don't have to worry when you work up a sweat or get caught in the rain."

"Great."

"And here." He hands me a sheet of paper.

It has the words *Changing Faces* and a phone number and a web address.

"What's this?"

"A group that might help."

I reread the words. Then I get it. "A bunch of freaks like me? Sitting around moaning?"

"It's a support group. It can help to know you're not the only one."

"Misery loves company."

"People find different ways to deal. You can learn."

"That's 'cause I'm smart. Aren't you going to tell me I'm smart, Dr. Ratner?"

He looks me in the eye. "You're smart, Sep. Good luck."

I skip Corina's party that night, of course. The party that would have been our coming-out party. Joshua texts me. I don't answer.

Then Devin texts me. "hey? u sick?"

I type: "vitiligo wins." And tears roll down my cheeks again. I delete it. I need to see her face-to-face. I type: "skipped school, thats all."

"u never skip school"

I type: "i did today."

"im about to go to the movies with C."

And she worried about me when she was waiting for her date? Good old Devin. I type: "have fun"

"thnx. hey, J just texted me. hes upset. whats going on?"

So that's it. I type: "forget it"

"oops, Cs here. gotta run"

"have fun"

"feel better"

It's funny Joshua would ask Devin for help. I'm glad now that I didn't tell her how bad the vitiligo has gotten. This month changed things; Joshua became the person closest to me. If my vitiligo had started after we were already together, he's the one I would have told. And now, if I was going to tell anyone that vitiligo has won, it should be him.

But I'm not going to tell him—so I'm not going to tell anyone. At least that way I'm not betraying him even more.

If this is crazy thinking, well, it's the best I can do.

And so the regimen begins. I buy tan and brown and olive turtlenecks. That way if some of the cream gets on them, it doesn't show that easily. Black and white were disasters. Luckily the weather has changed, and turtlenecks make sense now.

I put the seahorse stamp in my bottom drawer, along with the green ink. And I get a star stamp and blue ink. So that takes care of the back of my hand.

I wear my lipstick, of course.

And I paint the worm on my face with Dr. Ratner's miracle cream.

I am completely hidden. And better dressed than ever before. And I'm the one who thought vitiligo victims were ridiculous to go into hiding. In fact, I thought the word *victim* was melodramatic. I knew nothing.

I march to school in disguise. I march home in disguise.

No one knows.

For now.

In the first days Devin asked me a dozen times why I dumped Joshua. But then she stopped, like she just forgot it. She's too busy with Charlie. They text each other maybe twenty times a day. Maybe nine hundred. She doesn't have time to think about me.

Just like I was too busy to think about her the whole time I was with Joshua.

Guys do that. They slide into a girl's life like a thick layer of honey, blocking off the air.

Honey. I could smear myself with honey and go lie outside and see if Dad's fox comes to eat me.

He's still around, that fox. He ate Sarah's dead mouse

—when? God, it was three weeks ago already. I put it on a brick in the backyard, and the next morning Dad was so excited. He told all of us he saw the fox run up to the brick, snatch something, run halfway back to the bushes, stop to chew up the mystery meal, then disappear.

Mamma asked who put a brick in the middle of the yard. But I wouldn't fess up. I don't know why. These days I hardly talk, but I did then. I was happy then. I was with Joshua.

Anyway, Dad now leaves treats for Foxy on an irregular basis. He's convinced himself that the fox will come consistently if the food appears less than consistently. He thinks any wild animal will instinctively resist a regular food source that obviously isn't natural, otherwise they'd risk becoming tame, and tame foxes have no place in this world.

I don't know how Dad arrived at his reasoning. He's wrong. In Biology we're now on evolution and heredity, and Mr. Dupris told us canines are the earliest known mammalian carnivores. Mr. Dupris turns out to love foxes. One of his favorite experiments is by these scientists from Harvard who are studying foxes in Siberia. They've found out foxes can be tamed. No one expected that—they thought domestication had been bred into wolf-descended canines over centuries. But now they think a dog's sensitivity to human emotions has nothing to do with biology. Maybe it's just that when you aren't afraid of someone, when you don't have to fight them, you can understand them better. At least if you're a canine. Maybe this fox has Dad all figured out, and he knows that if he keeps coming around, Dad will put out food now and then.

Poor Dad. I think it's the fox who has tamed him. But I haven't told him; it would mean talking.

I'm grateful to know all this about foxes. I do my biology homework and then I do extra—extra reading, extra surfing the Internet. Biology is my lifeline. When I'm reading biology, I can pretend I'm still me.

I often watch for the fox now, though I've never seen it. I stand in the kitchen, drinking my new favorite tea. It has toasted rice in it, and the smell almost calms me. I bought it when I went with Rachel, of all people, to Chinatown in Philadelphia last Saturday. She's taking cooking and she needed ingredients for a Szechuan dish. I don't know why I accepted her invitation. Probably just out of surprise. Rachel is on a definite path: she'll be a science major in college, then go to medical school, then be a neurologist. Her father decided all that before she was born. So where this cooking class fits in, I don't know. Most of the kids who take it are not on the college track. Maybe it's just 'cause she loves to eat as much as I do, or as much as I used to. She talks about food like some people talk about love. Whatever. That's where I found this tea. It's Japanese and it's become my habit.

But Rachel is not my friend. I don't talk to her.

Devin and I walk to school, and others join us, but I've taken to eating a bagel as we walk, so my mouth is too full to talk.

I walk home with Owen on Wednesdays, but I make a point of not speaking. If he's noticed, he hasn't given any sign of it. He simply talks the whole time. I don't know why he doesn't simply walk alone. Being with me is no better.

And I don't know why Rachel invited me that Saturday. But when I didn't accept her next invitation, she didn't ask again.

Joshua texts me every night. It takes all my self-control not to answer. Once I wrote him a letter. Not an email message, a real letter. On lined paper. I kept changing my wording and having to start over again. Computers really are better than longhand. But I didn't want something electronic. I didn't want something repeatable. It was a one-time message. And I thought I finally got it right. I thought the words on the paper would make him understand, and make him feel better. Because I know he has to be a mess now. And that kills me. But then I ripped it up.

I can't go there. Just seeing there's a message from him

makes my chest squeeze so hard it hurts. Joshua Winer will never make me laugh again. We won't share food. We won't babysit Sarah. We won't . . . well, we won't anything. There will never ever be anyone like Joshua again.

I plague myself with questions. What if I told him? Would he dump me because I'm not beautiful? I don't think so. I think he'd do something worse. Stick it out with me and have to listen to all the nasty things people are going to say and just swallow his anger.

And his embarrassment.

Good God. I will never, never, never make Joshua embarrassed. Whatever is going to happen to me—and that's the real kicker in all this, I have no idea how far this will go—but whatever does happen, Joshua must not feel the fallout. This is my problem, not his.

And he deserves someone better than a blotchy mess.

I didn't contact the Changing Faces support group. I was going to. I went on the Internet to check them out. Then I found a blog called "I have vitiligo" and the big headline on it was "Vitiligo and Suicide." Teens wrote in about feelings of depression, thoughts of suicide. One guy called it "white leprosy." I found a YouTube video about a young man who committed suicide because he felt his vitiligo made him look like a monster. And I stopped.

I feel sorry for people who think about suicide. I really

do. But I don't want to know other people with vitiligo. Not until I'm strong enough to be able to help someone else, and not so weak I could be dragged down by someone else. So, for now, no support groups.

But I'm not alone. I have a fox. No boyfriend. No life. Just a fox. A fucking invisible fox.

32

TIGHTS, LEOTARD, BLACK SNEAKERS, black scarf. My face is blackened. I have on ears and a tail and whiskers. I pad into the kitchen where everyone else has gathered.

"Oh." Dad looks at me and his mouth stays open just a little. "Pina, you're so . . . grown-up."

"Yeah, a grown-up pussy."

"Dante!" Mamma clears her throat. But her eyes are on me, not him. "Well, Pina, you are eye-catching."

"No shit," says Dante. "She's going to collect the cat-calls tonight."

"That's enough, Dante." Mamma glares at him.

"I don't really understand why teenagers go trick-or-treating," says Dad.

"The guys do it for candy—and to get an eyeful of girls who flash their bodies, like Sep's doing tonight. You'd be amazed what low-cut costumes the most mousy girls put on."

"Your sister's isn't low-cut," says Dad.

"Nope. But Slut's still strutting her stuff."

"Stop it, Dante." Mamma drops onto a chair. "Just stop that kind of talk. Well, Pina." She shuts her mouth, though. Nothing else to say?

All right then. "If everyone is through, I'd just like to say thank you for the compliments." I take my tail and twirl it at them. "You've got your ordinary clothes on, Dante. Going as the imbecile you are?"

He pulls an inflated red balloon out of his paper bag. "Ta da."

"An imbecile with a balloon."

"My ball of fire." Dante smiles. "I look like an ordinary soul, but I throw fireballs."

"Pathetic," I say. And I take a paper bag with handles and go to meet Becca and Rachel. Devin is off with Charlie tonight, but we three girls will prowl together.

For no reason in particular, I go out the back door and turn my face to the sky and stand there a long time just letting the twinkling stars mesmerize me. The air is crisp but the cold we had all week has gone suddenly. No need for a jacket, which is good, because Dante is right: tonight I strut my stuff. Defiantly, in fact. Being in costume is liberating. Everyone's in costume tonight, not just me.

And I'm not just me. I'm a cat. A witch's black cat. If anyone crosses me, I'll put a pox on them.

I'm happy.

Stars are good.

Halloween is good.

I lower my gaze and happen to glance toward the rear of the yard when, oh, something goes across the grass. It's the fox! Our fox. And he's bigger than I thought. I bet he comes up to my knees. The very tip of his tail is white. He bounces through the dewy blades over to Mamma's fishpond and drinks. After a long while he straightens up and listens a moment, turns and looks right at me, then trots through the bushes.

He's gone.

He wasn't more than twenty feet from me.

Scraggly and wild. But he wasn't the least bit afraid of me.

I twirl around with both arms extended and the paper bag flying. This will be a brilliant night, I know it.

Becca and Rachel are waiting on the corner when I get there.

"Late," says Becca. She's wearing an Eagles football uniform. She looks very butch. But I don't think Becca is butch in the least. Maybe that's why she can dare to dress like that—she's got nothing to prove.

"I have a fox excuse." This is not true. I am late because I stood looking at the stars for a long time. But a star excuse is nowhere near as sensational.

"What's a fox excuse?" asks Becca.

"Foxy. He lives in our yard." That is also probably not true. But who can blame me if the excitement of the moment makes me exaggerate?

"They have fleas," says Becca.

Which is true. Red foxes typically take over woodchuck dens when they raise a litter. And woodchuck fleas torment them till the cold weather kills them off. But I don't tell Becca it's too late for fleas. That would mean talking more than I'm willing to.

"It's too late for fleas," says Rachel. Of course. She knows as much about foxes as I do—we're both in Mr. Dupris's class. She clasps her hands together in front of her chest. I'm not exactly sure what she's dressed as, but it's some sort of giant bug. She seems absolutely teeny inside those flopping wings and dangling antennae. Like a twelve-year-old. "Can I see him, too?"

"He doesn't stay in one place long."

"Don't be mean, Sep," says Becca. "If you've got a fox, share him with Rachel. She's an animal lover, like you."

And Rachel's looking at me, all hopeful.

"My dad has seen him a number of times," I say. "In the morning. But this is the first time I've seen him. Honest. I don't know when he comes around."

Rachel nods. "It must have been a fluke, anyway, because foxes aren't nocturnal. Something must have disturbed him."

"Maybe passing trick-or-treaters," says Becca. "Come on. Let's go gather the loot."

"I have something for you first." Rachel reaches in her bag and hands us each a little white half-moon.

Becca smells it and wrinkles her nose. "What is it?"

"Char sin bao. It's Chinese."

"Translate," orders Becca.

"Steamed bun with barbecue pork inside. Eat it."

Becca frowns. "Are you crazy, feeding us right before we're going trick-or-treating?"

"I made them miniature so we wouldn't fill up."

"You made this cute, smelly, little thing?" says Becca.

"Go on. Eat it."

We do.

Rachel's pointy face squinches in worry, watching us.

"They're great," says Becca in surprise.

"Delicious," I say. And it's true. I haven't enjoyed eating since I went into hiding, but right now I feel like I could eat a dozen of those little half-moons.

"All right, now we can trick-or-treat." Rachel actually leads the way to the first door.

We get candy. All sorts. And packages of microwave oven popcorn. And one house hands out old comic books, classics. They're in terrible shape or they'd be worth a mint. We eat as we go. I glance at the time; it's only 10 p.m. and I'm already puked out.

"Becca, is that you? Nice costume. And who's that cute little buggy and that hot cat?"

It's Tom Clements. He's on the football team. Trailing behind him are Martin Roper, Bill Brant, and Joshua Winer.

I stand stock-still. My body is leaden.

They're all talking but Joshua. He's looking at me. I manage to turn my head toward the street.

Then the girls go one way and the guys go another.

Except for Joshua.

And me.

I force a foot to take a step.

"Stay a second, Sep. Please."

I stand there. I am dead again. Why don't I fall?

"You look good."

In costume, I think. Covered.

"I miss you."

My tongue sits like a rotting, dead seal on the bottom of my mouth. I will cry if he says anything else.

This is bad. Very bad. I have to leave. I take another step.

He puts a hand lightly on my forearm. "I don't know what's going on. I think about you all the time. If you'll only talk to me, we can work this out. I know we can work this out."

"No," I say with that big, blobby, dead tongue. "Some things can't be worked out, Joshua. Forget me."

"You have to tell me. Not speaking is . . . God, Sep, it's wrong. You're wrong. This hurts."

I know. It's killing me, too. I'm wrong, so very wrong. But I can't find a way out that doesn't seem a lot worse.

I stand as tall as I can. "I'm sorry," I say. "Good-bye, Joshua." And I walk. One foot in front of the other. I walk away from the boy I love. I don't look back. I won't look back. I won't.

Becca and Rachel close forces around me, almost as though by some sort of instinct—the save-the-sister instinct.

Neither of them asks what happened. Neither of them has ever asked what happened with Joshua. But I know people think he dropped me. Who can blame them? He's Joshua Winer.

Still, I'm so grateful to them that they've never asked.

"Let's go on over to Baltimore Drive," says Becca. "The biggest houses are there. They give out the best treats."

I almost say it's late. But 10 p.m. isn't late. I want to go home. But I don't want to be alone.

Why is absolutely nothing easy?

"THE WORLD IS VISHNU'S dream." Those were the last words Ms. Martin said today before Becca took over Jazz Dance Club. I could swear she was looking at me as she said them. But maybe I just want to believe that. I'm still hoping for messages, answers, a way out. I'm still frightened out of my mind.

I walk home silent with Owen talking nonstop beside me. I don't even pretend to be listening. And he doesn't pretend to think that I am. He doesn't pause. He doesn't ask questions, not even rhetorical ones. He is simply voicing his thoughts in front of me. It dawns on me that he is utterly unself-conscious around me. Maybe around every-one? How? How did Owen get to be so smart?

We part at his corner and I walk the rest of the way repeating Vishnu's name so I won't forget it. But I don't say it out loud. I am not Owen. I am not that smart. I don't want others looking askance at me. I simply won't let that happen while I can still avoid it.

I hit the Internet, which has become my new home. I spend more time there than anywhere else.

Vishnu is a sleeping god. He lies on a giant serpent, an endless serpent, who floats in the universal ocean, the milky ocean. And he dreams. Everything that happens, everything we see and hear and smell and touch and taste and know, all of that is Vishnu's dream.

That time I met Ms. Martin walking Monster, she talked about another god, Lord Ganesh. Ganesh removes all obsta-cles. I read the whole story then, but I read it again now. Ganesh removes obstacles for a reason, an unforgivable rea-son. Shiva, his father, cut off Ganesh's head in a moment of anger, and then, when his wife had a fit, replaced it with an elephant head. What could be worse? But Ganesh somehow went on—he went through life with that ginormous head, that trunk, those ears, helping others, removing obstacles from their paths.

And all because of Vishnu. Vishnu dreamed the world,

so Vishnu dreamed that whole horror story. Vishnu created Ganesh's misery. And he can't make up for it simply by dreaming that Ganesh then does good for others. One act doesn't justify the other. I'd like to punch Vishnu awake and yell that in his big flabby ear.

Vishnu made a mess of his dream. Dad would call him a piece of work.

I am nine hundred times better off than Ganesh. Nine hundred zillion times. I still have my own head, the right size, with the right parts. Only the colors are different.

And I still have the same body.

"Your body is your animal." Ms. Martin said that today, too.

I try to know the experience of the animal that is my body. The most animal I've ever been is with Joshua. I remember that moment in lovemaking, when you cross the line from one kind of consciousness to another. A different sense of self.

I don't have that anymore.

But if I can believe Ms. Martin, people can get to that point of understanding themselves, of inhabiting the animals they are, if they can find a way to allow themselves passion and compassion.

Maybe that's what happened to Ganesh. That's why he could remove obstacles from others' paths. Maybe it had nothing to do with Vishnu. Ganesh could have taken control. He could have embraced passion and compassion and found a new way of being himself inside them, despite or because of that elephant head, it doesn't matter.

That's what I need to do. I can't just look to others to be kind to me. I can't control that. I have to learn how to be kind to myself. To the animal that is me. To this body. This skin. This me.

The rational part of me knows that this is the job ahead.

It sounds so simple.

The world is a giant deception. Hardly anything is simple.

I hit the off button.

IT'S THE SECOND SATURDAY of December.

I have been a zombie for ten weeks. The splotch on my face that starts at the top of my lips and used to look like a worm has been joined by a splotch over my left eyebrow and a series of spots on my right temple. The shape of it compares to nothing. It's a mess. My face is a mess. It's official: I'm ugly.

Fine. I wear my skin-cream mask. No one sees me. I'm safe for now. Who cares?

With the exception of that one visit to Chinatown with Rachel and the fiasco of Halloween, I haven't gone anywhere with anyone. Devin and I visit each other, but only after school at my house or hers. She's with Charlie on the weekends.

I'm over being envious of her. She has what she wanted: true love. I had it, too, though.

And I'm getting rich. I babysit a lot. Often twice a weekend. At those sweetly inflated prices. Last night Sarah told me her mother ate a child. Here's how the conversation went:

"Mommy ate a baby."

"Sarah, don't say such a crazy thing."

"She told me."

"She wouldn't say that."

"She pointed to her stomach and said, 'There's a baby in here.' "

"No, she pointed to her uterus."

"What's that?"

"It's a bag inside you that's meant to hold babies."

"Inside me?"

"Inside all girls."

"I can hold a baby in me?"

"Yes. But not now. Not while you're tiny. Ask your mother about it, Sarah. Ask her to explain."

So Mr. and Mrs. Harrison have benefitted from my babysitting. They're getting it on again. If I keep hiding like this, maybe they'll have a full house of little monsters. Then I could charge nine hundred dollars an evening. And all those kids wouldn't drive me crazy, because I'm already crazy.

I went officially crazy on the second Saturday of November. That was when our high school had the Homecoming dance. It was late this year, because our football team's match with our archrival wasn't until the last weekend of the season. And we always have the dance the night after that game.

Joshua and I had talked about going to the dance together. We had talked about me selling cookie dough with the cheerleaders and the Go-Camels, which is the support group for the football team. Lunatic mothers run it. They're all in love with their sons. They're the ones who sit on the bleachers and scream encouragement during the games even though the players can't possibly hear them. And fringy, moon-eyed girls are in it. I would have been part of it. Just to help raise funds for that dance.

Instead, of course, I didn't sell cookie dough. And I sure didn't go to the dance.

But Joshua did. With Sharon Parker.

He had to go. He's captain of the team, after all. And he needed a date.

But then he showed up at a party the next weekend

with Sharon. Devin told me. And he didn't have to have a date for that.

And Becca had another dance party, the Saturday after Thanksgiving, and Joshua went with Sharon to that, too.

Then this week Bill Brant tried to chum up to me at lunch. It was obvious: now that Joshua's not into me anymore, his friends are free to hit on me. I almost puked on Bill's sneaker.

Joshua's over me. He's with Sharon.

He's safe. That's what I wanted. Right?

Life goes on.

Joshua's safe, safe, safe. He has someone else to turn to. Someone waiting in the sidelines. He can forget. He has Sharon.

All I have is me. This is what I wanted, and I have it, and I hate it, and I'm burning up inside.

Life goes on. How dare it?

Which is why I am now standing on one foot with my other leg cocked, the bottom of the foot pressed against my standing leg's thigh. This is tree pose—*vrksasana*. It's a balance challenge. Ms. Martin says the point of this pose is not balance; the point is to find other relationships within the body—other relationships that will support you. I need other relationships to support me. I can do this.

Life goes on.

I hold the pose a full three minutes on each side, which amazes me. Then I walk into the bathroom and scrub my face clean and look in the mirror and repeat that thought: life goes on.

And I'm sick of being mad. I can't control vitiligo. I'm not normal. So what? This is my life. It's taking a shape I never would have planned—but it's mine. It's all I have. I can be a tree; I can find a way to support myself on one foot.

It is Saturday night. Life goes on. It is December. Life goes on. Christmas is coming. Salvation Army bells and decorated trees and Christmas carols and lasagna and red and green and silver spangled days. Christmas. When everyone is happy with the greedy thoughts of presents ahead.

Presents.

Anyone deserves a Christmas present. I'm going to give myself one. Now. Tonight. It's been over a week since the last spot appeared. Maybe this is who I'm going to be. But even if I keep getting worse, tonight feels right. The me I am in this very moment is ready. I declare that—silently, but firmly.

Dante and two friends are watching the third X-Men movie. This is, of course, the nine hundredth time Dante has watched it.

I walk down the stairs slowly. No cosmetic cream. No stamps on my hand. No lipstick. And I'm wearing a shirt with a regular neckline and no scarf. I am a mutant, like the characters in the movie. So it's fitting I should arrive like this.

I stop a moment midway on the stairs and stand absolutely still. In mountain pose now, tall as I can be. I breathe deep. I feel my body's weight. Anger dissipates. All I feel is the strength inside me. I can do this. Tim and Zach and Dante—I can face them.

I descend to the bottom step and look at my hand. It's white, but not just the spot. It's white all over because I'm gripping the banister so hard. Fuck this shit. That may become my new mantra.

I walk in. The lights are off, of course. What a brave girl I am, to expose myself to the dark. I almost laugh. I sit down on the couch beside Zach.

"Hey, Sep," says Zach.

"Hey," says Tim. He's on the floor with his back leaning against the coffee table.

"What do you want?" asks Dante. He's in the chair.

"I just came to see the movie."

"You hate this movie," says Dante.

"No, I don't. Not anymore."

"You can't stay," says Dante.

"Why? Are you guys going to make out or something?"

Zach laughs. "Who cares, Dante? Let her watch."

"Come on, Sep. These are my friends."

"You're just watching a movie. I won't say anything."

"You're already saying things."

"I'm just answering you."

Dante stands up. Then he sits down. "Okay, you can stay. But only if you go make us popcorn."

"All right."

"All right?" Dante sounds so surprised he just might faint.

I leave and go make popcorn in our old hot-air popper. But not just ordinary popcorn. I sprinkle it with garlic salt and grate parmigiano on top. It smells fantastic. I carry it back.

Tim turns on the light.

I'm stunned. I thought I had till the end of the movie before I'd be exposed. But here it is. Now.

I put the bowl on the coffee table.

"What's on your face?" asks Zach.

"Skin."

"No, you've got something white on your lips and smeared across your cheek. And your forehead and temple. And neck. And hand . . ." His voice trails off.

"It's skin," I say.

No one speaks.

Tim finally takes a fist of popcorn and stuffs it in his mouth. "Great," he mumbles.

"I've got vitiligo," I say. "It's a skin condition. It gives me white marks."

"So what do you have to take for it?" asks Zach.

"Nothing. It's just there. It doesn't hurt me."

"And it's not contagious," says Dante quickly.

"Will it go away?" asks Zach.

"Probably not." I take a single popped corn and mash it flat in my mouth. It sits on my tongue like a mangled, pregnant Communion wafer. "Do I look like a monster? One of your mutants?"

"It's not so bad," says Zach. He looks at the popped corn in his hand. "My cousin got burned with acid, and he looks a lot worse than you."

Dante leans forward. "Shut up!"

"It's okay," I say. "I need to hear it, Dante. I need to be prepared for what people will say."

Everyone's silent.

"Sep?" says Tim at last.

I look at him.

"With your tits and ass, you'll always be hot."

I have to clench my teeth not to cry. Maybe my molars are going to get filed down to nothing with all the pressure

I've put on them lately. "If you're trying to get me to fuck you, Tim, forget it."

Tim and Zach laugh; Dante doesn't.

"Oooo," says Tim, "the mouth on you. I never knew you spoke like that."

"I never knew you did, either. You're lucky Dante didn't punch you." I look around. "So are we going to watch the movie or not?"

Tim turns off the light.

I sink to the floor and sit beside Dante's chair. That wasn't so bad.

Okay, these boys have known me practically all their lives. Certainly all their lives that they remember. I've made them peanut butter and jelly sandwiches and poured them glasses of milk since they were five and I was seven. So they're not an accurate picture. They care about me. Strangers will be different. I've read about it.

But I have to start somewhere.

"HEY, DEVIN."

Devin smiles at me, then her face freezes, then she catches hold of herself and smiles harder. "How you doing, Sep?"

"I've got vitiligo."

"I know," says Devin. But I can see from her face that she never guessed how far it had gone. And she had no idea how revolting it would be.

"Now everyone will know."

"You look good."

"Don't say that. I haven't yelled at my mother for trying

to be nice for over a month now. Don't make me yell at you."

"Okay." She grows visibly taller. The way she lifts her sternum and brings her shoulder blades together in the back, you'd think she had been doing Ms. Martin's yoga asanas.

"You're my fellow warrior," I say.

"What?"

"It's a yoga thing. Don't worry about it."

"No bagel today?"

"I already ate."

We march side by side. It's Monday morning.

As we turn the corner, Becca joins us. She stares at me. "What happened?"

"I have vitiligo. It's a skin condition. It's not contagious. It gives me white blotches. All over. You should see my chest. No, you shouldn't. It'll probably never go away. It doesn't hurt. It isn't degenerative. I'm not dying. I didn't do anything to make it come. I can't do anything to make it go away. It's not the same as being albino. My hair and eyes won't change. Or at least my eyes won't and probably my hair won't. Any other questions?" I talked a mile a minute.

Becca nods slowly. "Wow." Then she snaps her fingers. "The lipstick! That's why you started with the lipstick."

"You're an Einstein, Becca."

"Look, the way to handle this is to tackle it head-on. You know, grab it and smash it to the ground."

"I know what a tackle is, Becca. Remember Joshua?"

"Yeah." And her eyes grow huge and blaze up. "Hey, did he dump you because of this? That piece of slime!"

"No. He doesn't know. We just split."

"Why?"

I should tell her it's because I acted like a shallow piece of slime myself. But I don't want to deal with the way the two of them would rally against such self-deprecation. "It's personal."

"Well, anyway, tackle it. This thing. Viti—what?"

"Vitiligo."

"Right. Let's tackle it. We can give you a nickname. That takes away the chance of people coming up with one on their own. Zebra. How about zebra?"

"I don't want a nickname. If people call me names, fuck 'em."

Becca winces. But she says, "Right. Fuck 'em." She blinks.

It's funny who wants to be a warrior for you. I'm stunned, and grateful. But I can't bring myself to say thank you.

I get through the morning with a lot of stares, but a minimum of questions. Lunch is a bitch, though. People ask. I get tired of answering. I have my warriors—I might as well use them. So I tell everyone to ask Devin and Becca. And I eat my eggplant parmigiano. It's delicious—one of Mamma's specialties. I'm glad my taste for food has come back. Rachel did that for me—on Halloween, with her little Chinese steamed buns. It was like she pressed a toggle switch back to on. Lunch is a good thing.

Speak of the devil—Rachel appears and sits down across from me. She stares at me while I eat. I am about to tell her just to ask Devin, when she says, "That's eggplant parmigiano, isn't it?"

I nod.

"Your mother's trained you. You know good food. Here. Eat this." She puts a little plastic container and fork in front of me.

I open it and blink fast. The smell is sharp. "What is it?"

"Cold sesame chicken with scallions. Eat it."

I nearly laugh. "You're becoming a tyrant, the way you order people to eat things." But I take a bite. "Oh my God."

"Do you like it?"

I finish the whole thing and pass the container back to her. "Fill it again for tomorrow."

She glows. "I'm going to be a chef."

"Better. You're going to be a goddess to gluttons everywhere."

Well, how about that? I'm not the only one bleeding

internally these days—I bet Rachel's parents are almost dead they've been bleeding so bad. A chef, and why not? Fuck neurology.

The afternoon passes. And the evening. And the night. I lie here in bed and clutch my sheet to my chin. I came out today for real—not just to Dante's friends, but to everyone—out of the vitiligo closet, and I haven't dissolved or exploded or otherwise vanished. I am alive.

Tuesday doesn't go as well. I can see it coming before it actually gets here. I'm walking home alone and three girls are walking on the other side of the street, eyeing me. They're sophomores, I'm pretty sure, because I recognize one. They cross to my side and my stomach closes around a cold stone, like oyster nacre around a grain of sand. Only I don't think pearls will be the outcome.

"What's the matter with you?" asks one of them.

"Vitiligo," I say.

"Is that some Italian word? Your mom's Italian, right? Is this some foreign disease?"

I want to answer her, say something, anything, but words won't come. I want to shrug at least, but my shoulders won't move.

They walk ahead of me, silent, and turn at the corner.

"Everyone said it was awful up close, but it's worse than awful."

I can hear them, and they know that. My hand goes to my cheek—to the tomato-worm splotch.

"Like someone dropped her in an acid bath."

I think of Zach's cousin, the burn victim. My hand works its way up my temple and across my forehead. So many splotches.

"She should put on makeup or something. It's disgusting to go around like that."

Then they're too far away for me to make out their words.

I stop still. My breath comes quick and shallow and for a second I think I'll suffocate, just fall and die. But then the dizziness passes. I catch my breath.

And I stare after them, my hands in fists. *Disgusting*. The word hisses inside my head.

I knew it was coming. I dreaded it. But it's still hard to believe. Their eyes . . . good Lord. They looked at me like I was a monster.

I can imagine doing any number of things right now. I could rend my clothes and scream and roll on the sidewalk. I could shout obscenities or throw bricks from that pile in the yard over there.

But I don't.

And I won't.

I uncurl my fingers and my hands drop heavy. Those

girls can't reduce me to raving. I'm not a monster. I'm me, Sep.

Though right now, as this pain washes over me, I feel like a wounded beast.

I felt that way earlier today, too, when I saw Joshua in the lunchroom. I looked away fast. I don't know if he saw me. But he has to know about my vitiligo by now. He has to be curious as to how bad it is. He must have looked at me.

And now he knows why I asked him to turn the lights out.

Joshua. I wipe my face off and walk slowly now. Joshua Winer.

The worst thing is, sometimes I wonder if our whole thing together ever happened. I mean, of course I know it did. But maybe it didn't happen the way I remember it. Maybe I'm totally crazy and I made up the kisses, the sex. Maybe I'm some pathetic, deluded thing. Joshua Winer with me? It is unbelievable.

When I think like that, I want to slap myself. That's the old me—the one who put labels on people—who thought of him as Mr. Cool. Joshua Winer was with me, for real and true. Because he's a real and true person. Not just a popular football guy.

I get home and I can't do my work. Well, everyone

needs a night off. I sit in the backyard, wrapped in a blanket, and hope Foxy will come. But he doesn't.

Wednesday slogs along. Nothing new. Until after Jazz Dance Club. Melanie's sitting on the bench in the locker room when I get out of the shower.

"You're not hiding anything anymore," she says. "So you don't have to be the last one to shower anymore."

Her directness would be offensive, except it isn't. She's just being honest. "I guess it's habit now."

"Break it. Those old habits need to be swept away."

And that anger I've been controlling so well comes burning up again. "What do you know about it?"

"Lesbians face some of the same stuff. Ever since you came to school all natural on Monday—no makeup or lipstick or anything—I've been thinking about you. Nonstop, really. You have it easier in some ways."

Whoa! "Exactly how?!"

"No one believes you chose it, so no one can blame you. But people are always coming up to me and asking why I don't act right, just act right." She snaps her fingers. "Like that."

"But people don't have to know it about you. It can be your private thing. It's not tattooed on your face."

She smiles, but her lips give her away. They quiver just a little, like before you start to cry. "That's why I tattooed it on my ankle."

The inside of my nose goes all prickly. It was a brave act, that tattoo. "Solidarity."

"You bet."

"But you're in control. You can put on socks and hide that tattoo and no one gives you a second look."

"I do sometimes. But most of the time I want to shout out: 'I'm a lesbian! Get over it!'" She stretches out her legs, and crosses them at the ankle and points at her tattoo, and gives a little laugh. "A quiet shout."

I walk to my locker, towel dry, and pull on my clothes, fighting self-consciousness about my blotches. Melanie's still there. I can feel her eyes on my back. I go suddenly lightheaded. Weird. Almost frantic.

I turn to her, completely dressed now. "Why did you say, 'Think pink'? You know, months ago, you said it to me. Maybe you don't remember, but you said it. Think pink."

"I've been waiting for you to ask." She leans toward me. "You know the pink ribbons people wear? To raise awareness about breast cancer? The Think Pink Foundation makes them. My aunt got cancer and moved in with us during her chemo, so my mom filled our house with pink junk."

"I'm sorry. About your aunt, I mean."

"Don't be. She's doing good. She moved back to her farm in Lancaster months ago. But what I want to tell you is my aunt became a nut about pink and she taught me. Here's how it works. If you stare at pink long enough, then take it away, everything looks green. It's some trick of the eyes." She smiles. "Anyway, green is hope. You seemed so sad, I wanted you to have hope."

"Why? Why would you care?"

She walks over and we stand face-to-face a moment. Then we both move a little closer, and she kisses me. Melanie kisses me on the lips.

I knew she would—in the instant before it happened, I knew. I let her. I yield as though it's the most natural thing in the world. Soft and lovely.

But then I step quietly away. "I'm not into that, Melanie."

"Do you really know what you're into?"

There's no doubt about it: I'm aroused. But I want Joshua. I want Joshua so bad. "Yeah. I do. I really do." I put on my jacket and head for the door. Then I stop. Hell, why not be honest? "Thanks for the kiss."

"Anytime." She's stuffing things into her backpack; she doesn't even look up.

"You want to walk with us? Owen and me?"

"Nah." Her voice is light, and I can't detect sadness in her. She looks strong. And wonderful.

A strong and wonderful person who gave me the first kiss I've had on these naked white lips. "Thank you. Really."

She turns her head, still leaning over her pack, and her eyes crinkle. "You're welcome." She grins. "Really."

I walk out and Owen's waiting for me. Faithful Owen. He smiles at me and either he's pure of heart or he's a great actor, because I don't see even a flicker of pity in his eyes. Owen is the best.

He starts talking automatically, like he's that windup bunny in the battery commercials. All about math. Just like he's done every Wednesday for so long.

"Owen," I say.

He stops with a loud intake of breath. "You spoke. You actually graced me with your words. Well, one word."

"Tell me, what do you do on Wednesdays? What keeps you after school?"

"I organized a club. We talk about the environmental movement that's circling the globe, the one Wangari Maathai started."

"Who?"

"Maathai. She won the Nobel Peace Prize for getting people to plant trees in Kenya."

"Trees? A peace prize for trees?"

"Trees combat erosion and offer shade and building materials and fruits and barriers to keep wild animals from your herds, and the list goes on. If you have trees, life is good, and when life is good, you don't need to fight. Trees lead to peace."

"So you plant trees?"

"No." He smiles. "We talk about planting trees."

I manage a smile back.

"And in the spring, we're going to landscape that big, ugly dirt field beside the elementary school, where they used to play soccer before the new field got set up."

"And then the elementary school children will stop all their wars?"

"They might."

I laugh. I actually laugh. And Owen's the one who got me to do it. "What do you call your club?"

"The Green Club."

Green. A convergence of green. A serendipity of green. A splendid lushness of global green. I'm not mystical, no no no. But this is just too much. And my motor's still running from Melanie's kiss. I halt and twirl in place.

Owen takes a few more steps, then notices I'm not beside him. He stops and faces me.

I rush up to him and realize with surprise that he must have grown a few inches in the last couple of months, because my head barely reaches his chin as I hug him hard. Then I step back.

He steps toward me.

I put my hand up. "That was just a thank-you."

"Well, you're welcome. And, Sep." He clears his throat. "You can thank me any time."

My body is electric. But it's not Owen I want. Still, something has happened. Somehow I know I'm going to want someone again someday. I will not spend the rest of my life missing Joshua Winer.

But I mustn't hurt anyone else even by accident. Owen is real. "I hope I didn't confuse you. It was a burst of gratitude. But the last thing I want is to confuse you."

Owen smiles. He says nothing. But his eyes tell me everything.

36

MELANIE'S AUNT IS RIGHT. The pink-green connection turns out to stem from visual afterimages. If you stare at pink for ten seconds, then look elsewhere, you'll see green—the afterimage. It's an optical illusion. I found a website that demonstrates it, called the Lilac Chaser. Pink dots move in a circle, and you stare at a black cross in the center. Pretty soon you see only one green dot moving in a circle. The cool thing is, there never really is a green dot. But the eye "sees" one.

I don't know if it matters whether there's a green dot. I mean, if you perceive it, how different is that from what it really is? We act on what we perceive. It's the best we can do.

On Thursday after school Jazz Dance Club meets again for a rehearsal. We're performing between acts in the Battle of the Bands tomorrow night. I get there early and the only people in the gym are Becca and Ms. Martin. One look tells me they're arguing. I lean against the wall and try to be inconspicuous.

"We practiced last weekend," says Ms. Martin, which is true. We had two practice sessions, one Saturday morning and another Sunday afternoon.

"It isn't enough. We aren't ready." Becca's arms are crossed at the chest. But now she drops them and her whole body cries defeat. "This is going to be a big fiasco. You should have let us practice after school all week. This is going to be so bad."

"Too much practice—"

"How can you keep saying that!" Becca shakes her head. "You're the one who makes us do the same yoga poses a zillion times."

Ms. Martin puts her hand on Becca's shoulder. "Dance isn't yoga, Becca. With yoga you do it over and over and over, striving for perfection. But a dance performance is different. You have to practice it enough that your body can do it without thought, but not so much that your body can do it without heart. What you want is organic. The girls know their parts. You've done a good job leading them. The audience will enjoy watching you."

I'm totally alert. I had no idea Ms. Martin really cared about dance.

"Whatever. It's too late now. We can either cancel or dance." Becca looks down. Then she looks over at me and her face changes. "All right, then, I'm rearranging the floor plan. Sep and I will be center front and the rest will be in three small groups at each side and the rear. And that means . . ."

She goes on explaining the changes all this will make in the choreography, and Ms. Martin is agreeing, and the girls are coming into the gym and I'm waiting by the wall, suspended on those words: *center front*.

I've become a good dancer. I'd have to be an idiot or an even worse liar than I am not to admit that. I changed this fall. It's not like I'd go out and tell every girl who wants to dance that she should get laid, but I really believe sex woke my body up somehow—and now it's got some new level of awareness or plane of existence or whatever it is people say when they talk about these things. I simply know my body better now. So it makes sense Becca would want to try to focus the audience's attention on the two of us. But what will my face look like under the spotlights? Our costumes cover our arms and legs—but our faces are exposed.

Becca explains the new layout to everyone. I can't meet anyone's eyes when she tells where she and I will be, but no one objects, and we rehearse and it's good. Becca's changes actually make the whole dance better, regardless of who starts out center front and keeps returning to center front and ends in center front, center front, center front. We are dancing to Gnarls Barkley's song "Crazy," and I am loving, I am loving, I am loving the way he begins his lines over and over again till he gets to his point. I think I know what he's talking about, too. I know exactly where he's been, because I've been there. And right now, with *center front* ringing in my head, I feel like I could go there again.

In the locker room, I go up to Becca. I wipe the sweat off my forehead and stand straight. "About makeup . . ."

"I knew you'd do this." Becca slams her locker and turns to me. "We're all wearing lipstick. We're all wearing eye shadow. Whatever else you want to do to yourself is your business, Sep. The audience will be looking at your moves, not your face." She leaves. And I can hear the words she didn't say lingering in the air: *so get over it.*

Sure. I can do that, sure. But what's the point of making

the audience have to get over it? The parents and friends and little brothers and sisters and the kids in the high school who haven't seen my face before—what's the point of making them have to go through the surprise of vitiligo before they can pay attention to the dance?

Except maybe if they do see my face and then I dance good—really good—they'll forget my face. Wouldn't that be something. Our dance is short and fast-paced; it's just a few minutes really. Is that long enough to win their attention away from my naked face to my moves?

Can I dance that good?

Friday after dinner, which I really can't eat, I pull my hair into a ponytail and look at myself in the mirror. It's just the Battle of the Bands, but I feel like I'm going to war. Like the soldiers in Vietnam in the book Owen gave me. I've read it three times already. Lieutenant Jimmy Cross made them slog on through the incessant rain, despite the mud and the lack of visibility. They didn't want to, but they did it. I know what I have to do.

I scrub my face and leave my skin cream unopened.

We're all supposed to meet in the actors' makeup room down the hall from the auditorium at least a half hour before the show starts, so I walk to school. That way Mamma and Dad don't have to wait so long. Dante said he'd come, too—with Tim and Zach. And Devin will be there with Charlie. And Rachel said she'd come. Owen didn't say anything, but I know he'll be there. So that's it—I've got my cheering squad.

I put on my costume in the girls' locker room and go crowd into the actors' makeup room. Everyone's joking, but their eyes are haunted. The MC calls the first group to go arrange themselves on the stage behind the curtain and the second group to line up in the wings, ready to run on after the curtain drops and the first group gets off. He leaves with those two groups.

Jazz Dance Club is all here now. Lipstick and eye shadow and costumes. None of them give me any weird looks. No one in the makeup room gives me any weird looks. Everyone's too worried about themselves.

The big clock over the wall of mirrors says the show has started. Someone undoubtedly is saying some sort of welcome and thanking the long list of people who helped make this all possible and all that. Then we can hear them. Trumpets blasting. Pretty bad, I think, but who can really tell from here? The first band now clatters into the hall and the rest of us in the makeup room strain to hear: Is anyone clapping?

Things go fast. The third band has already left the

makeup room. There are nine competing bands. That's a lot. A ton. Jazz Dance Club performs after the fifth band, to break things up.

Now the fourth band is called. Then the fifth. Then Jazz Dance Club squishes into the wings.

The band that goes on before us calls itself Blue Man Group, which seems like it might not really be legal, but they do it anyway. They're three guys and one plays the drums while the two others try to fit together candy-cane shaped pieces of PVC piping, which is supposed to be a drumbone (whatever that is) but keeps falling apart, so the two guys give up and bash each other with the pieces, laughing like idiots. The drummer stays with it, though. At least the audience is prepared for failure now, so that's good. And the audience actually claps at that total fiasco. Yes, this is a good audience. I look around and my eyes meet Melanie's in the dark. She gives a quick nod.

The curtain comes down and we take our places and it goes up again. I can't see anything past the lights that glare up at us. I can't see my cheering squad. Or anyone. Anyone else who might be out there. And anyone might be out there.

I feel stupid. Like I've entirely forgotten the routine. I can't even remember how it begins.

But the music comes on strong and my body moves the second it does. Bang, just like that. We're all moving, fast and furious. The back I count on rolling across is there, right on time. And the bodies Becca and I have to weave through are all there, right where they should be. Arms and legs and feet and hands, everything pivoting and rocking and kicking and flying. All that matters is this elbow jab and that moon roll and these kicks kicks kicks. Everything clasps where it should and releases at just the right moment, with the rhythm of the music and the beat of our hearts and the hum of the universe. Galactic wonder!

It ends. Music gone. All we do is pant now, pant and sweat.

The audience is clapping and hooting and stamping their feet and we somehow realize it's time to bow. Deep, over and over. The lights go off and for a split second I can see into the crowd, but I close my eyes and listen to the thwack of the falling curtain. I let myself be ushered away into the wing and out into the hallway.

I danced my ass off. Better than ever before. I ran up and down the spine of that endless serpent, I swam in the milky ocean, and whether I shook Vishnu awake or not, I am awake. That's what's important. It's great, this being awake thing, this dancing thing. It's sensational.

With or without an audience.

Over the next week the realization slowly sinks in. Dance is it for me. This semester I've learned so much and, while I still love math, I'm pretty sure I want to be a biologist who works on animal behavior. But I'm going to dance all the rest of my life, till I drop from old age. Dance holds body and soul together.

Yesterday was Christmas. In a week, we'll be in January. Joshua Winer's birthday is in January. I don't know the day. He never told me. But I want to do something nice for him. I ended things so selfishly—protecting myself, not him. It's time to do something decent.

And I'm strong enough to do it now. I've danced naked-faced in front of strangers. And I can stand on my head for as long as I want—yoga's sinking in. I laugh sometimes, too, especially with Owen. And Devin and Rachel and Becca.

So I go on the Internet and find a copy of *Blue Moose*, by the author who wrote Joshua's favorite children's book, and I order a copy mailed to him. It feels good.

37

IT'S SNOWING. THE FIRST snow of the season. Dad talks about how weird this is. How when he was a kid snow started before Thanksgiving. Winter is shrinking. But it's not gone. And, oh, I love this snow. I take some in my hand and I literally love it. I feel goofy.

There's a male cardinal in the spruce tree. On one of those ugly bare lower branches that a gust of wind has already swept the snow from. He's brilliant scarlet. And I love him, too. In fact, I'm in love with him.

I go inside and wash my hands, and I'm in love with the water that gushes from the spigot. And the soap. And the towel. And the towel rack.

Owen and I go sledding. Each in our own aluminum disk. But one time he invites me in his, and he circles his arms around me and we slide and swirl. I know he's wanting more. And I know I have to tell him it won't work. I can't just talk about some vague kind of confusion. Sometime soon I have to explain point-blank that I don't like him that way.

The next day I make the most delicious pea soup with Dante. We stand at the kitchen counter and chop side by side. Carrots and onions and celery and cabbage and potatoes and tomatoes. It's perfect, looking out the kitchen window at the snow. I wonder where the fox is now.

"You know, Dante," I say, "I'm okay these days."

"Yeah," he says. "So?"

"So you can stop being nice to me."

"No shit? I can torture you again?"

I laugh.

"Okay, Slut. I'm out of here. You finish." And he leaves.

But I don't even care. It's more normal this way.

I dump the rest of the chopped vegetables into the pot and put a lid on and talk Mamma into watching it while I go to the mall. I need a long walk right now. It's just too beautiful.

I fall in love with every car that passes. With every telephone pole. And when I finally get there, with the whole busy parking lot.

Slinky's selling perfume to a man. Oh, I know her name is Carey, but somehow the name Slinky is still in my head and it's not bad to let it stay, now that I know the label means nothing. Slinky leans toward the man. I eavesdrop. He buys two bottles.

When he leaves, I say, "You're good at that."

She turns to me, her mouth opens and stops slack for a second, then on she goes into a big smile of welcome. "Merry Christmas. Or belated Merry Christmas. Or early Happy New Year."

"It's called vitiligo. Do you want me to go through my whole speech about it, or will the name be enough?"

"Does it hurt?"

"Not the way you mean."

She raises an eyebrow. "Is it dangerous?"

"You won't get it. And I won't die of it."

She taps her fingers thoughtfully on her lips. "It's an interesting challenge."

"Forget it. I'm through with makeup. No lipstick, no nothing."

"Good. That's a good decision."

"Is that a mother's approval or a professional cosmetics clerk evaluation?"

"Both. This way you're unique. Can I sell you shampoo, then?" She smiles and there's a wicked glint in her eye. "I

have some that will make you smell like vanilla. Appropriate, no?"

"I bet you don't sell any of that to your African-Amer-
ican customers."

"You lose. Vanilla is popular; everyone likes to smell
like a pound cake. Or a pumpkin pie. Want pumpkin shampoo? Or eggnog? Oh, yeah, how about eggnog shampoo?"

"Are you trying to get me eaten alive?"

"Eaten, huh?" Slinky leans across the counter and
whispers, "Did you bed the football hunk?"

"I never called him a hunk."

"But he is, right?"

"That's ancient history."

"Are you sad about it?"

"Some parts of it. Not all."

"Hmmm. So who are you in love with now?"

"Did I ever say I was in love with the football guy?"

"High school girls are always falling in love."

I grin. I wonder if Slinky knows what a genius she is.
"I'll take a bottle of vanilla shampoo." I'm already in love
with it.

Slinky rings up the sale and hands me the bag. "You're
pretty, you know."

I hold my eyes on hers. It takes a few seconds before I
find my voice. "Thanks. So are you."

"I mean it."

"I do, too."

She waves. "A mutual admiration society. Don't be a stranger."

The next day Mamma and Daddy go into New York City on the train. They leave early. And Dante disappears on me again. He took the you-can-stop-being-nice-to-me declaration to heart.

Just before noon the doorbell rings. I open it.

Joshua Winer stands there.

Tears spring to my eyes. But it's just a physical thing. I'm not sad. In fact, my pulse races. I can hear it inside my temples. "Hello, Joshua."

"I got the book. Thank you." His eyes take me in. I can tell he's really seeing me for the first time since I've been out of the closet. A steely determination runs along the line of his jaw.

"Oh. It came fast," I say. "I meant it for your birthday."

"Yeah, well." He's wearing his jacket—the same jacket he wore in fall. It was too heavy then. It's too light now. His hands are deep in his pockets.

"You must be cold." I step aside. "Come in?"

He comes inside and I shut the door behind him.

"I hope you like the book."

"I read it already. It's great."

"Good." I look down at his sneakers, dripping snow on the floor. "Want some pea soup?"

"No. Thanks. Here." He pulls a small, skinny package out of his pocket.

"What's this?"

"Your present."

"It's not my birthday."

"It will be someday."

I open the present. It's a flat pen, unlike any I've ever seen before. I read off the side: "Strawberry Red? What is this?"

"Henna Penna. It's natural coloring for your lips. I know you're not covering up anymore, but in case you ever want to add a little color just for fun, this is an easy way. And it lasts longer than lipstick."

Now tears do come, real tears. I blink them back. "You're with Sharon now."

"Yes."

I put the Henna Penna pen in my pocket and force myself to smile. "How's that working out for you?"

"Good."

"I'm glad."

He turns to go. Then he stops. He looks over his shoulder at me. He shakes his head. Then he turns to face me again. "I was furious with you for so long." He lifts his hands, then shoves them in the pockets of his jacket so hard, I'm surprised the cloth doesn't rip. "Not at first. At first, I was just a mess. You dropped me, like snapping your fingers. Poof. I was gone. Banished."

"I'm sorry."

"Yeah, well, Sharon helped out. She's complicated, and . . . I don't know, but she's got this way of coming through when you really need her."

I do my best to smile. "That's good."

He gives a little laugh. "Whatever. Anyway, then you came to school without makeup, and I saw what had happened, and I understood. That's when I got furious." His fists are still pushing against the inside of his pockets and I can see the outline of his knuckles. He looks down a moment and when he looks back up again, his eyes shine with anger. "You had no right, Sep. You treated me like a jerk. Like some superficial asshole."

I blink at the word. This isn't how Joshua talks. "I protected you."

"I didn't ask to be protected."

"I cried a lot."

"I could have cried with you."

"I shouted a lot."

"I could have shouted with you."

"I was afraid of that. Afraid you'd regret it all later."

"You can't know that. I don't even know. I'll never know. You didn't let me find out. In your great quest to find the true Sep you robbed me of any chance."

I wipe away tears. "I'm sorry."

"It's like you decided who I was. And I hated the person you decided I was. And it made me wonder if that's who I really am." He shakes his head. "You messed with me."

"It wasn't that. You deserved better, Joshua."

"See? There you go again. Figuring out what I need. What I want. Who the hell gave you that right?"

"No one." My voice comes like a high-pitched squeal. "And it's not true anyway. It's me I disappointed." Tears come, but I swallow and keep talking. "I was afraid you'd stick with me out of chivalry. I couldn't stand the idea of seeing pity in your eyes. I put all that on you and I'm sorry. I put it on you . . . because . . ." I stop to swallow my tears. " . . . because I wanted to dump me. Can you understand that? I was so mad at myself for getting vitiligo—for not being able to do anything to fix it. It's me I couldn't love. Not you. You're good and I know you're good, and I think that made it even harder. You were too good for me." I'm wiping fast but the tears are coming faster. "I wish I hadn't shut you out. I wish I hadn't been so self-centered and stupid. I was wrong. I'm really sorry, Joshua."

"Good. That's all I wanted to say." He lets out a long

breath. "No. No, it isn't. Did you know? Did you know from the start? Did you set out to use me? To have your little fling before this skin thing got too bad?"

I can't speak.

"'Cause that stinks worse. Other people have feelings, Sep. I have feelings. There's more to life than just your pain."

I nod. The tears stream and I wish I'd dissolve. "It was . . . mixed up. The best thing in my life and the worst thing in my life were happening at the same time. And they got locked together. I know you got hurt. I hurt you—I know that. I'm sorry. I'm sorrier than I've ever been for anything ever in my whole life." I'm wiping the tears and the snot, but everything keeps coming. "Is that all now?"

"I think so. I'll come back if it's not."

"I'll be here. Joshua . . . ?"

"What?"

"I loved you. I love you."

"Well . . . thank you for telling me. I'm glad you told me. Next time you love someone find a better way to show it." He shrugs. "One last thing."

I cringe inside.

"I'm not that good. Maybe you just saw what you wanted to see."

And he's gone.

I sink to my knees and lower my forehead into the puddle left by his shoes.

I was lousy to him. Wretched. And he is that good, no matter what he says. I should have been good, too.

But he's all right now. He made it through. He's happy with Sharon. I'm glad he's happy with her.

I go to the kitchen and come back with a rag to clean up the floor. Then I look through Dad's jazz CDs and put on Louis Jordan.

I go into the living room and dance. It's not like Jazz Dance Club, where we have the whole gym, so we can run and leap and kick like maniacs. But there's still plenty of room to move. And I love moving like this. Subtle and soft. It isn't compulsion. I'm not a swift anymore. I'm not a tuna.

Joshua didn't say he loved me back.

There could be nine hundred reasons why he wouldn't say it. But the fact is, he didn't.

But someday someone will. Someone will love me.

And I will let him.

I will love him back good next time. Like Joshua said, I'll find a better way to show it.

I drop onto the couch and fall back into the cushions. I don't want to be alone right now. I want to be with a friend. Not a lover. A friend. And I know a friend who probably wants to be with me.

I use the phone, of all things. Texting has its limitations.

"Hello."

"Hello, Owen." And I suddenly realize I never thanked him. "Thank you for *The Things They Carried*."

"You liked it?"

"I keep it under my pillow.

"That sounds good."

"Are you free?"

"Sure."

"Hungry?"

"Sure."

"I have pea soup."

"I love pea soup. And I'll show you a video clip on the Internet, about this mathematician-dancer, Karl Schaffer, who works algebra into his floor patterns."

"That sounds great."

"It is. I've been surfing dance sites ever since your dance performance. This one is perfect for you."

I swallow. "There's something else, Owen. I have to tell you something."

"What?"

"I like you, Owen. I guess I love you. But I'll never be your girlfriend."

A moment of silence.

"So?"

"So do you still want to come over?"

"Do you really have pea soup?"

I can hear the smile in his voice. I laugh. "Hurry up. It'll be ready by the time you get here."

Thanks to Eva, Robert and Barry Furrow, Suheily Aponte, Sarah Babinski, Brenda Bowen, Dan Consiglio and his students in the U.S. Literature class at the Nueva Esperanza Academy of Philadelphia in 2008–2009, Libby Crissey, Nikyyah Cruz, Dena Davis, Alice Galenson, Sarah Geselowitz, Sally Hess, Annette Hoeksema, Abby Holtzman, Mimi Huerta, Britany Johnson, Samara Leist, Grace Leonard, Zaida Melendez, Rosa Mykyta-Chomsky, Rachel Platt, Kristina Pratts, Juan Ramos, Natasha Santiago, Jeanette Shaw, Richard Tchen, Talia Tiffany, Robert Velez. Thank you to Margery Cuyler, for believing in this story. And a special thank you to Melanie Kroupa, with her very sharp mind and pencil.